CHARLIE WILCOX

CHARLIE WILCOX

SHARON E. McKAY

Stoddart Kids
TORONTO • NEW YORK

Published in Canada in 2000 by
Stoddart Kids,
a division of Stoddart Publishing Co. Limited
34 Lesmill Road
Toronto, Canada M3B 2T6
Tel (416) 445-3333 Fax (416) 445-5967
E-mail cservice@genpub.com

Published in the United States in 2000 by
Stoddart Kids,
a division of Stoddart Publishing Co. Limited
180 Varick Street, 9th Floor
New York, New York 10014
Toll free 1-800-805-1083
E-mail gdsinc@genpub.com

Distributed in Canada by
General Distribution Services
325 Humber College Blvd.
Toronto, Canada M9W 7C3
Tel (416) 213-1919 Fax (416) 213-1917
E-mail cservice@genpub.com

Distributed in the United States by
General Distribution Services
4500 Witmer Industrial Estates
Niagara Falls, New York 14305-1386
Toll free 1-800-805-1083
E-mail gdsinc@genpub.com

Canadian Cataloguing in Publication Data

McKay, Sharon E.
Charlie Wilcox

ISBN 0-7737-6093-8

I. Title.

PS8575.A2C47 2000   jC813'.54   C99-932564-7
PZ7.M33Ca 2000

Cover and text design by Tannice Goddard
Cover illustration by Julia Bell

*We acknowledge for their financial support of our publishing program the
Government of Canada through the Book Publishing Industry Development
Program (BPIDP), the Canada Council, and the Ontario Arts Council.*

Printed and bound in Canada

To my father, Ian (David John) McKay,
who would not let me forget that
Charlie had a tale to tell. And to my mother,
Dorothy, who is a Wilcox after all.

"Do what's right with all your might."
— CHILDREN'S BEDTIME VERSE

Acknowledgments

I'd like to thank the Canada Council writer's grant program, for their financial assistance in the creation of this book.

Dr. David Parsons, of St. John's, Newfoundland, who was, and continues to be, a fountain of information. Without this dear, brilliant man, this story would have neither depth, nor insight into a tragic time in Newfoundland history. And my thanks also to his wife, Dr. Daphne Parsons, who must have exercised a great deal of patience at the sight of her husband spending a ridiculous amount of time researching and e-mailing this far-away writer.

Keith Wilcox and Audrey Wilcox Grenier, son and daughter of Charlie, who understood the spirit of the story.

Barbara Berson, whose encouragement I could not have managed without.

Kevin Major, Newfoundland writer, for his suggestions.

Captain Howard D. Chafe, Royal Newfoundland Regiment, St. John's.

Mrs. Elsie Percy, Librarian, Brigus, Newfoundland, and her daughter, Beverley Percy, R.N.

The Spracklins of Brigus (Dulcie, Walter, Lorne, and Daphne).

ACKNOWLEDGEMENTS

Irene Rabbitts, Brigus, Newfoundland.

Janet Story, Archivist of the Lillian Stevenson Nursing Archives Museum, St. John's, Newfoundland.

The War Amps, Ottawa, Canada.

Linda McKnight, Westwood Creative Artists, literary agent.

Lynne Missen, my editor, whose patience and thoughtfulness won the day.

To those who offered their editing skills and encouragement: Erika Redman, Ylva Van Buuren, Plum Johnson, Philippa Campsie (*merci*), Gail Tilson, Ian Rogers, Catherine Bonham.

Patrick Crean and Pat Kennedy, whose efforts launched the book.

At the end of the day, and every day, my husband, David MacLeod, and our sons, Sam and Joe.

In memory of John Northway Leamon, Brigus (1921 to 1997).

And the people of Brigus for treasuring what is theirs to keep, forever.

Hu?

Chisels, angishore, muddle, what does it all mean? Newfoundland has a language all its own. Flip to the back of the book, to the *Did You Know?* section and all will be explained. To learn more Newfoundland words, consult the *Dictionary of Newfoundland*, published by the University of Toronto, Ontario, Canada.

Chapter 1

MAY 1915

"Charlie. CHAR-LIE."

Lucy Wilcox shaded her eyes with her best wooden stirring spoon, a *muddle* she called it, and peered down the road.

He couldn't have gone far, it wasn't past seven in the morning.

"CHAR-LIE." Lucy yelled again, and then clasped her hand over her mouth. It wouldn't do, yelling like a fish-wife.

"What is it, Lucy?"

Eliza Norton charged out of her own pink clapboard house and stopped short.

"It's come." Lucy waved the telegram in the air.

"I'll be right over." Eliza darted back into her house.

"CHAR-LIE." Where was he? "Emma, Emma," Lucy

1

turned and called down the hall of the house. "Emma, Emma." Deaf as a haddock that one, but no sense trying to replace her. Emma was a Fields and there had always been a Fields working in a Wilcox house.

No Charlie, no Emma. Lucy sighed. Fish-wife be damned (although Lucy was not one to curse — not out loud anyway).

"CHARLIE."

Claire Guy, herself on a mission to deliver eggs to Mister Pinkstone, stopped in front of the garden gate.

"I saw Charlie go up Grave Hill, Missus Lucy," said Claire with great authority. Claire, at thirteen years of age, prided herself on knowing the goings-on of everyone in Brigus.

Lucy grabbed her heart. "Oh, Claire, don't jump out at people like that."

"I didn't. I was just . . ."

"Never mind. Go and fetch him. And if you see Skipper Sam, ask him to come home, too," said Lucy.

"But, the eggs . . ."

"Yes, Missus Lucy," Emma burst through the door and stood beside Lucy. One black braid, thick as a rope, hung over her shoulder.

"Emma, I'm going to pack Charlie's things. Take this." Lucy handed Emma the muddle. "Stir the soap. I should never have started that today. And when you're done with the beds, take the carpet from the sewing room outside and give it a beating. Claire," Lucy looked back out to the road, "you still here? Run along. Now, Claire."

"Where's Charlie going?" Emma asked, which is just what Claire wanted to know.

But Lucy Wilcox was gone. Down the hall she went and was swallowed up in the dim of the great house.

Claire walked through the village. She came to a small drawbridge, leaped over the loose planks, and landed on those that were not. And there was Skipper Sam, walking dead straight for her.

"Morning, Skipper. I'm looking for your Charlie. Missus Lucy wants you home, too. It's important," said Claire, smartly. "Charlie's going somewhere, I heard Missus Lucy say so. Is he going to Canada?"

Skipper Sam's eyes narrowed and his hand went to his cropped, salt-and-pepper-speckled beard. He leaned back against the railing of the footbridge. "Never you mind. Go on then, find Charlie."

Well, Claire was miffed. She wasn't to get any more information from Skipper Sam, not this day. Claire set out again, this time toward the wharf. The sun was up, the water crystal clear, the day would be warm. In the distance Claire could hear the ping of a hammer from the smithy's shop, the sound of the water lapping up against the shore, and the squawk of seagulls. The smell of the cod was strong, even if the run was over.

It was a busy place, Brigus. The busiest port in all of Newfoundland. It was said that, in the year of our Lord nineteen hundred and fifteen, more quintals of fish were landed here than any place on earth. And yet Brigus was still little more than a village, streets that looped up and around and back. Picket fences, pebble walks. Tiny draw-bridges crossing mirror silver brooks. All one had to do was drop a line and there'd be a fat trout just begging for the fry pan. There were two fine ponds in the middle of the village, for swimming in during the warm months and skating on during the cold ones.

"Jim," Claire hollered to Jim Norton, who was heaving a hard rubber ball against the side of a wall.

"Yea?" Jim hurled it again and spun around. "What?" The ball shot up into the air. And like the ball itself took aim, it came down and smashed right into Claire's basket of eggs.

"Yowl!" Jim leaped up in delight. "See that, see that?"

"How dare you. How dare you!" Claire shook with rage. "Look, they're all cracked. You did this on purpose, Jim Norton."

"I did not." Jim didn't even have the good grace to hide his delight.

"Yes you did," Claire sputtered.

"Ah, Claire, I did not."

"Yes you did. Now I have to go home and get more eggs and Missus Lucy wants me to go fetch Charlie from up Grave Hill because he's going to Canada and . . . ." Claire stopped short. She was near to tears. Great gobs of egg dripped through the basket and landed like yellow bird droppings on the rutted, sandy road.

He was in for it now. "Tell you what, I'll get Charlie." It was the least he could do.

"What's he going to Canada for?"

"I don't know. Maybe to Montreal to live there for good." Claire turned and marched back the way she came.

Jim Norton shoved the ball into the pocket of his knickers, straightened his cap, and set off toward Grave Hill. He was the same age as Charlie, going toward fourteen years old. Just think on it, soon he'd be out, finished. No more school for him, boy. Wasn't he, even now, mucking out, grooming the horses, and driving his father's carriage? Soon they would have an automobile, too, the first in Brigus. Jeeze, he'd drive that too, maybe. But Charlie, what could poor Charlie do? Not much with a club foot. Maybe that's why he was going to Canada to live.

Jim kicked dirt ahead of him. Funny they called Charlie's foot a *club foot*. It didn't look like a club; after all, the foot was still there — it was just pointed and turned in, pigeon-toed like. It didn't lie flat so Charlie had to walk on his heel. Charlie said he wanted to go down to the Labrador for fishing and to the ice for sealing. Skipper Sam was Charlie's father, so maybe he could. But Charlie wanted to sail with Bob Bartlett, too. Captain Robert Bartlett himself, no less. What could Captain Bob do with a cripple?

Jim skipped past ol' Missus Cotton's mint-colored cottage and ran a stick across the white picket fence that hemmed in weeds. He gave the long, thin reeds that poked out between the slats a swat.

"I see you, Jim Norton. Hit my bushes again and the next thing that switch will hit is your backside." Missus Cotton hung her thin, gray face out the second-story window and hollered bloody murder. Jim made tracks. Missus Cotton was always cross on account of having lost a husband and both sons to the ice. Frozen solid, all three. Mind, that was near twenty years gone. Jim thought she might have cheered up a bit by now.

Jim headed up the hill, past the old walled-up graveyard where, a long time back, Marg the Indian woman was buried with her baby. Up he went into the heathland but not so far as Rockwell Kent's place. He was an artist and in trouble with some townsfolk on account of his speaking German. They were at war with Germany, so it wasn't a good idea to speak German, not loudly anyway. Not the way Rockwell Kent did — at the top of his voice from the cliff's edge.

Jim could see Charlie's blond hair, just. He was lying against a rock, his face to the morning sun.

"Charlie, wake up." Jim flopped down beside him. "What are you doing?" As Jim was dark and lanky, Charlie was fair and small.

"Watching," said Charlie. He yawned and ran his fingers through strands of blond, tufted-up hair.

A small forest of masts stood moored in the harbor on this calm, soft day. In the middle of the bay, a schooner glided across the water and above it a gull kept pace. Rats of the air, thought Charlie. That's what his mother called gulls, hated them she did.

"Look." Charlie pointed to a small pile of rocks directly in front of them.

"What?" Jim looked down. "What is it?"

"Bend down and look." Charlie giggled.

Jim crouched down on his haunches. Sure enough, there was something embedded in the rocks. A small gold bit was sticking out.

"Look through it." Charlie rolled his eyes.

Jim put his eye to the gold bit, looked, and leaped back.

"A spy glass. Where'd you get it?"

"It's my father's."

"You took Skipper Sam's spy glass?" Jim near swallowed his tongue. What'd it matter that Skipper Sam Wilcox was

Charlie's own father, it was the finest spy glass in Brigus, maybe the whole of Newfoundland. Jeeze, you just don't go taking a thing like that!

"I didn't take it," Charlie was miffed. "I borrowed it. Besides, it will be back before anyone knows it's missing."

Jim whistled under his breath.

"Look again. You can see all of Conception Bay, you can see almost everything."

Jim took a second look. It was true.

"So, why'd you take it?"

"I told you, I didn't take it. It's mine anyway. Well, it will be one day. I'm going to inherit it. Father says so. So I'm just borrowing it from myself. And I'm going to put it back — just as soon as it comes in."

"What comes in?"

"Bartlett is coming in sometime this week," said Charlie. No finer captain sailed out of these parts than Captain Bob, except maybe his own father.

"Are you sure?"

Charlie nodded. "Miss Bartlett heard it on the wireless."

Well if Captain Bartlett's own sister said it was so, then it was so.

"Look down there. There's Phil and Clint." Jim had a keen eye.

"Where?" Charlie pitched forward and peered through the glass.

It was like this, Clint Miller and Phil Jackson were bullies. More than bullies. They were Charlie's own personal bullies, like God had set them down right here in Brigus just to torment one Charles Wilcox.

"Charlie, they see us."

"Do not. They're too far away."

"We should go. Besides, your mother wants you home," said Jim. "You are going to Canada to live. Montreal. Don't you have an uncle in Montreal? Maybe you'll go to a hockey game."

"Montreal?" Charlie reeled back.

Saying it out loud made Jim think. The two had been together forever, even their mothers were best friends. Brigus would not be the same without Charlie.

Jim shrugged. "Get the glass out of there and let's go."

"I can't take it out and put it back. It's stuck in dead tight."

"You can't leave it here."

"Only for a while. I'm going to sit here all day and wait."

"But your ma wants you."

Charlie pondered. "OK. I'll run home. You stay here and guard the spy glass."

"I don't know . . ." Jim dithered.

But it was too late. Charlie, for all his hip-hop disability, raced down the hill at lightning speed.

Chapter 2

" Charlie Wilcox, where have you been?" Eliza Norton, Jim's own mother, marched down the road toward him, skirt swaying, arms flapping. Charlie stopped dead in his tracks and met Missus Eliza near eye to eye. She wasn't a big woman, not like his own mother. Missus Eliza was tidy-like, neat and little, like a spry pony. But her voice was big and she'd think nothing of giving Charlie a trimming. Just like her own son, she would say. Charlie wished she didn't care for him quite so much.

"Your mother has half the village looking for you, Charlie Wilcox. You get home this instant. And have you seen my Jim?"

Charlie's eyes dropped like a bullet. "No." It was a lie, of course.

"Off then." Missus Eliza shaded her eyes and looked up, then down, the sandy, ribbed main road of the village.

Charlie bolted for home.

He hadn't far to go, just down the road a bit. Charlie's home was a large, two-story, cranberry-red clapboard house with white trim. Most of the houses in Brigus were covered with clapboard. Most were painted yellow or blue, light green or white. Most were one or two stories high, with gently slanted roofs — any more of a slant and an Atlantic wind would take them off with one good blow.

Charlie skirted the front door, ran around to the path, and ducked low under a window. He could hear his older sisters, Ethel and Jenny, saying good-bye. They were off to do rug hooking for the church bazaar. The front door slammed and all was quiet. Charlie ducked low, hip-hop, under another side window and slipped into the backyard. His foot was no bother, none a t'all.

"Charleee, where've ya bin?" Big Emma Fields, with a fat wooden clothespin stuck in her mouth, stood amongst white sheets that bellied in and out. They hung from a clothesline that stretched from the back house to a neglected outhouse. "Your moder and fader 'ave been lookin' for ya. Ooo ma be in ome trouble." Emma slid the clothespin around in her mouth. He could see, even from that distance, that it was getting juicy.

"What'd I do?"

"Ann't tell ya." Not that she knew a darn thing, but why tell Charlie that? Emma plucked the soggy peg from her buck teeth. "But, it seems to me," she paused for effect, "that you're not doing your chores."

"Did so. Fed the dogs, brought in the coal."

"But did you beat the carpet?"

Charlie looked at the carpet hanging over the back fence. "Beating the carpet's your job."

"Now didn't I hear your mother tell ya to help out." It was a long shot but Emma gave it a try.

"Mother didn't say nothing about beating a carpet." Charlie glared at Emma.

Emma returned the stare but then shrugged. Pity he was thirteen years old. It was lots easier to get him to do her bidding last year.

"Besides," said Charlie, "I'm going to Montreal. And I'm going to stay with my uncle on Dorchester Street and he's going to take me to a moving picture and a hockey game."

"Montreal? A moving picture?" Emma near turned pea-green. Well that explained Missus Lucy having her knickers in a twist. Her precious baby was going away.

"Maybe they're sending you away 'cause you're useless, 'cause you don't do your chores. Better get the water then, and that's no foolin' or maybe they won't want you back. Ever." Emma grabbed the wicker laundry basket and stomped into the house, black braid and all. She didn't mind being the maid, after all, there wasn't much a sixteen-year-old could do in Brigus besides gutting fish, but honestly, putting up with Charlie was almost more than she could bear.

Charlie grabbed two buckets, plus the water hoop, and crept back down the side path to the front of the house. He crouched under the back parlor window. He heard something, something that made him stop, might have been his mother's voice but the window was closed dead tight.

Charlie put one bucket down, tipped it over, and stood

on it to look through the window. Through the wavy glass, with only the odd air bubble, he saw the strangest thing — his mother and father holding each other! Oh, he had seen his father give his mother a hug at Christmas, even a kiss once, which sent all three children into a fit of laughter, but this was different.

His mother's face was buried in his father's chest. Her shoulders heaved up and down. She couldn't be crying? Charlie teeter-tottered on the pail. He could see his father's big hands around his mother, patting her back, thump, thump, real gentle. Why?

"What are you doing?"

Charlie near fell on his head.

"Jeeze, Claire, wear a cow bell or something, would you?" Charlie scrambled off the bucket.

Claire giggled.

"I'm to get the water. And then I'm coming back home because I'm going to Montreal," said Charlie. He picked up his buckets, and hoop, and headed for the road.

"Yes, I know," Claire smiled the smile she practiced in the mirror. "Can I help you fetch the water?"

"What for?" Claire Guy was a pest. She had a face like an egg, smooth and flat, and eyes like pies. And her hair was always a mess of curls. They jiggled even when she was still, which wasn't often.

"Well, it doesn't matter because I have to find Jim Norton," said Claire. "He smashed all my eggs this morning and my mother says he has to pay for them. Have you seen him?"

Charlie knew exactly where Jim was — up on Grave Hill guarding the spy glass.

"Can't say I have." Charlie ran off, in his fashion.

CHARLIE HIP-HOPPED down South Road, then up to North Road. The water trough was in front of Lambe's butcher shop, near the Convent of Mercy where the nuns lived, and beside St. Patrick's School. He plunked a bucket down and twisted the tap. A silver ribbon of fresh water thumped against the bottom of the bucket.

"Charlie boy," Mister Lambe stood fat and round under his butcher sign. "Have you been to your home? Your mother is looking for you."

"Yes, Mister Lambe." Charlie filled up the second bucket, plopped them on either side of the hoop, then stepped in the middle just as Mister Norton's horse-drawn taxi-wagon pulled up.

"Hello there, Charlie," Mister Norton slowed the horses. "Have you been to your home? Your mother's after asking for you."

"Yes, I've been home."

"Good man. And have you seen my Jim? His chores are waiting."

Still up at Grave Hill, thought Charlie, and he gave a little prayer. He shook his head, not daring to speak or look Mister Norton's way. That was two Nortons he had all but lied to this morning, plus Claire. Charlie stepped into the water hoop, which kept the buckets from banging against his legs. He pulled it up to his waist and lugged the lot back down North Road.

"Hey, Hoppy-boy, need a hand, or a foot?"

Charlie winced. Clint Miller and his sidekick, Phil Jackson.

"Hey, Hoppy-boy, cod got your tongue? Or your foot?" jeered Clint. The two boys laughed hardy.

Ping. Ping. Two pebbles bounced off the buckets.

"Hey there, peg-leg, step on it." Clint doubled over with laughter.

"Shake a leg," cracked Phil.

Clint and Phil had a repertoire of ten or so insults. Sometimes Charlie could wait them out, ignore them, but not today. He dropped the hoop. He turned, slowly, scanning the street for anyone, anyone at all. Charlie weighed his options. Stay and fight, or run?

"Well, look, do ya think the sissy is going to fight? All on his own?" One side of Clint's mouth turned up in a sneer. His eyes were black and marble hard. "Where is your little pal?"

Charlie stepped out of the hoop and away from the water just as Phil landed a rock right on the pail. Jeeze, not only did it tip over but one of the buckets looked split.

"You're a case, Phil," snarled Charlie.

"Where's your mammy? She goin' ta come save her little cripple?" Clint stepped closer, closer, closer still.

"Yea, and you'd look right good getting whipped by a woman," said Charlie. Was calling his mother *a woman* bad? He wasn't sure but it didn't sound right.

"Ya stupid little beggar." Clint closed in on Charlie and gave him a shove. Charlie stumbled backward and landed on his butt and elbows. It didn't take much to land Charlie in the dirt. He was half the size of both boys and with a club foot — well, he was never too steady anyway.

Charlie rolled over and chopped Clint off at the knees with his foot. He yelped, then fell like a tree. They don't call it a club foot for nothing. In seconds Clint was back up on his feet. He leveled his foot at Charlie's backside and took a swing. Missed. His foot hung in the air. Charlie rolled again, snake like, and knocked the other foot out from under him. Again, Clint hit the ground with a thud.

"Bloody little beggar," Clint snarled. And again, he was up on his feet in no time. "Think ya got me? Hu? Hu? Hey, takin' a nap there, Hoppy-boy?" hissed Clint.

Before Charlie could get on his feet, Clint, his fists clinched so tight they looked like potato spuds, popped Charlie again, right in the mouth. "Look at that, look at that!" Clint squealed. It was no more sport than fishing in a barrel.

With two hands on the ground, Charlie pushed himself up and stood on two shaky legs.

This time all Clint had to do was give Charlie a shove. Down he went again. Charlie didn't so much as let out a whimper. Bite his tongue off, he would, before he'd let Clint get the better of him.

"See that," laughed Clint. "Nothing to it." And he laughed some more.

"He's all in, Clint," said Phil. "He's had enough." Phil spoke like an automobile running backward — all grunts and gut-sounds. He came over from England when he was little. Much as he tried, the English accent wouldn't leave him.

"What'ya mean?" Clint looked Phil's way.

"I mean he's had enough. Let's go." Phil looked over his shoulder. His mother would be in the garden this time of day. If Phil was caught teasing a little kid, ya could be sure he'd be hammered within an inch of his life. Besides, truth was, Phil thought that Clint sometimes took it too far.

"Hey, Clint?" Charlie stood behind him, ready.

"Wha . . ."

Pop. Charlie's fist met Clint's nose. Dumb luck. You would near hear the blow. A gush of red blood spurted from his nose.

"You . . ." Clint dabbed his face and stared at his bloody hand.

Charlie cowered down. Honest to God, he didn't mean to give him a bleeder. Jeeze, he was as good as dead.

Then came Lucy Wilcox. Storming down the street, wearing a face like thunder. Her blue print dress, almost hidden by a kitchen apron, fluttered around her ankles, her white lace collar at her throat was just a little crooked.

Clint saw her coming, too. "You're nothin' but a stinkin' angishore, Charlie Wilcox," hissed Clint right into Charlie's ear. Clint covered up his bloody face with his sleeve and the two boys beat a path down the road.

Charlie's mother spoke not a word, not one single word. With one hand she pushed a stream of loose black hair back into a thick bun. The other hand reached down, right there in the middle of the street, and yanked Charlie up onto his feet by his ear.

"Yeoooo," Charlie howled like a cat.

"Where have you been? I have been looking for you for two hours."

It's not as if she wanted an answer, and certainly Charlie was too busy trying to keep his ear attached to his head to give one. It was a sight — watching the two coming down the road.

"The buckets . . ."

16

"Never mind the buckets," said Lucy. "We have plenty of water."

In no time they landed on the gallery of their own house.

"Into the kitchen. There's a bath waiting," said Lucy.

Charlie rubbed his ear. "Why do I need a bath?" This made no sense. Surely he wasn't to go to Montreal this very day!

"Bath."

"But . . ."

"Did you not hear me? I said into the bath — now." Lucy peered down at him.

And another thing, his mother hardly ever got mad. But she sure was mad now. Why? Going on a trip was a good thing!

Chapter 3

The kitchen was warm and smelly. Emma stood at the stove stirring the soap. The stink of the mixture of old fat and lye was enough to put off a cat.

"Your bath is waiting, your worship," said Emma, and not nicely.

Charlie stuck his tongue out at her, which Emma didn't see. Which was just as well. Emma packed a wallop.

"Go away," Charlie snarled.

"Don't talk to me that way, Charlie Wilcox." Emma waved the wooden muddle in the air. She might be sixteen, and the maid, but she didn't have to take any lip from anyone — Wilcox, Bartlett, Norton, Leamon, Guy, Spracklin, or none. Founding settlers indeed. As if it mattered. Thought they were all too good for the likes of the Fields. Ha!

"That's enough, Emma, and you, too, Charlie," Lucy came into the kitchen holding Charlie's Sunday church clothes. "Emma, run down the road and pick up Charlie's buckets. Off you go."

Emma stormed off in a huff. Bad enough she had to work like a horse, but picking up Charlie's water buckets was just too much. She'd be glad to get married and get a house of her own. Maybe Murphy Milford was a bit thick, but he was steady. If he asked her on Saturday at the Church Social to marry her, she'd say yes.

Charlie ducked behind the screen that surrounded the bathtub and flung his clothes onto an old wicker chair that sat by the corner of the tub. He dipped a toe into his bath. Not too hot. He dropped into the lukewarm tub that squatted on four fat paws near the big, open fireplace. Towels hung in the chimney corner alongside dog irons and shiny copper cooking utensils. Winter or summer, it was the warmest, snuggest place in the house.

"What were you fighting about?" Lucy came around the screen, picked up the washcloth, and ran it over Charlie's back. She was the lady of the house, part of Brigus society, but her hands were big and strong. Still he was thirteen, that be going toward fourteen years of age, too old to have his mother wash his back. This was no time to remind her of that, thought Charlie.

"Emma and I weren't fighting."

"I was not talking about you and Emma. I was talking about you, and Clint, and the Jackson boy."

"We weren't fighting, just knocking about."

"Let me see your lip." Lucy took hold of Charlie's chin and tilted his face toward her.

19

"Pardon me?" Lucy looked him square in the eyes.

"I hate them." Charlie tucked his chin into his shoulders. His lip was swelling but it didn't hurt much. Not like last time.

"They're two sleeveens, sure, but that's no matter. You're not to say *hate*. Hating is a heavy burden to carry and there's no reward in it." Lucy scooped and dumped a pot of water over his head.

"Then I dislike them more than anything or anyone in the world. What do I need my hair washed for?" Charlie rubbed his eyes with two balled-up fists.

"What were you fighting over?"

Charlie shrugged. Another pot of water came splashing down over his head.

"Mother!"

"Did they call you names again?"

Charlie shrugged again.

"Did they say something about your foot?" Lucy looked at the poor turned-up foot soaking in the water.

"I can take it."

Lucy sighed and sat back on the creaky wicker chair.

"Charlie, I have something to tell you," said Lucy.

"I know. I know all about it." Charlie squealed.

"What do you know?" Lucy was surprised.

"I'm off to Montreal to stay with Uncle Stephen. And he's going to take me to a moving picture and hockey game. And . . ."

"Charlie, where did you get that imagination? You're not going to Montreal." Lucy bent down and dumped yet another pot of water on his head.

"But . . ."

"A telegram came early this morning." With a wipe of her hands, Lucy reached into her apron pocket. Out came a yellow letter with bold blue type across the top. "It says here that you are to check into the General Hospital in St. John's by 4:00 p.m. today. In two weeks' time you'll have your foot operated on."

"No Montreal?"

"No."

Charlie thought on that and then, "Yowl!" he squealed, yet again.

Finally, finally, he'd be as fast as Jim. As for Clint and Phil — just let 'em try and catch him.

Better yet, and Charlie tried not to think on it too much, he'd be able to go to the ice, and if he could get a berth, to *sail* with Bartlett himself.

"Wait, Charlie, it's not that simple."

Charlie sunk under the water and scrubbed his blond head. Up he popped, then under again.

"Charlie," whispered his mother, "I . . ."

Charlie bobbed up and down, howling, laughing. Water ran over the lip of the tub and formed little puddles on the floor.

"Charlie, you're making a mess." Lucy squeezed out the washcloth, stood, and walked to the sink. She'd talk to him on the train. As it was, they had precious little time.

"So, the bad copper has turned up." Skipper Sam stood at the doorway, holding a small leather valise.

"I have, Father, and I'm off to the hospital." Charlie stood and ducked his head around the screen. He leaped out of the tub and reached for the towel to give himself a rub. His grin went from ear to ear.

"There's not much time," said Sam, who was really a captain. "Eliza sent this valise over, Lucy, and I got you both railway tickets — first class for my two world travelers."

"Oh, Sam, you didn't. This will put us back . . ."

Sam put his fingers to his lip and Lucy stopped talking. The hospital stay would cost a small fortune, a dollar a day for twenty, maybe thirty, days. And then the cost of the operation was on top of that. But the price was not to be discussed, not in front of the boy.

"I'll just go and get changed," said Lucy. "Charlie, put on these clothes and mind the water. The towel is getting wet." Lucy near ran out of the kitchen.

"Here, my son." Sam took the towel and gave Charlie's head a rub.

"Father, what's the matter with Mother? First she's mad, then she's not, then she's mad again. What did I do?"

Sam pulled up the old wicker chair. "Your mother's not mad," he said. "She's just nervous."

"About what? This is what we wanted."

"Charlie, she's your mother. You are leaving home for a month or more and going to a place that scares her a bit. Not that there's anything to be scared of. No, no. You'll be fine. You're just her little one and, well, that's how mothers are. And . . ."

"And I'm an angishore."

"Don't say that, Charlie."

"Well, it's true. I heard 'em say it. They say, 'Charlie Wilcox is a good little fellow even though he's a poor little angishore.'"

"Charlie, they don't mean it. There's nothing sickly about you, not now anyway. But you have to realize that we near lost ya a hundred times when you were a babe. It's a God-given miracle that you are with us now."

Sam looked around the kitchen, high and low, as if the cooker or the kitchen irons would tell him what to say next. "There, back there. See that shoe box behind the stove? That's what you slept in. Jeeze, you were a mite — nothing to you. A seven-month baby, they called you. So small, Charlie. All balled-up, like a cooked shrimp. I could hardly touch you — that afraid of you I was. You hardly looked like a babe at all."

"I was pink." Charlie giggled.

"No, not pink."

"Blue then." Charlie had heard about blue babies.

"No, not blue," said Skipper Sam, softly like. "See-through."

Charlie looked down at his arms and hands. "See-through?"

"Yep. We could see every vein in your little body. And your heart, Charlie, it pumped so hard, so very hard."

"How hard? Like it might pop out and fall on the floor?" Charlie howled with laughter.

"You're a rascal, young Charlie, give me that towel." Skipper Sam gave his son's hair a rub.

Charlie looked into his father's eyes, which were gray, the color of fog rolling across the bay. The kind of eyes you could look into, and into, and into. His eyebrows were bushy and his eyelids folded in on themselves in the corners. His beard was black and gray mixed together. And it wasn't all straggly like other folk, it was always trimmed and neat. He was a spiffy dresser, that was sure. And another thing was sure, Charlie loved his father, no more than his mother — he loved both more than life itself. Charlie pulled on his underwear, then his pants.

"It was a cold winter you were born into," Skipper Sam carried on. "We kept you on the lip of the stove to keep you warm. And your mother, she sat in that very chair over there and watched you, rocked you, day and night. There were times when I thought it was her will alone that kept you alive, Charlie. They said you would die, but she said no. She fed you like a kitten, you were too weak to suck. And she talked to you, day and night. The Parson, he was always at our door. Every morning expecting to find a little corpse."

Skipper Sam leaned back in his chair and muffled a laugh. "I mind the time she chased him away with that wooden muddle of hers. Your mother, a God-fearing woman, chasing the Parson out of the house armed with a spoon." Skipper's deep laugh rocketed around the kitchen. Nothing could be wrong in the world if Skipper Sam was laughing. "Here's your shirt, son, and pass me the hairbrush."

"Father, I'm too old to have you brush my hair." Charlie made a grab for the brush.

"Are you about to deny your old father a pleasure?" Sam took the brush. "Now, that's how it was. Your mother loves all her children, but it was you that she fought for from the beginning." Sam ran the brush over Charlie's hair, parting it first one way, then another. Neither looked very good. "And she did fight, Charlie. Can't think of how much linseed meal went to your chest. And now she has to let you go for a bit. Try and be patient."

Charlie gave a solemn nod. "I will, Father."

"There, a more handsome boy there never was." Sam leaned back and admired his hair-brushing handiwork. Well, it was the best he could do. The child had hair like hay.

"Now, we'll get your mother and head down to the train station. Pity your sisters aren't here, but they didn't know and no sense calling them home now." Sam gave his son a pat on the back and strolled out of the kitchen.

Charlie looped his suspenders over his shoulders, picked up a home-knit stocking, and carefully rolled it over his up-turned foot. His foot didn't look all that bad. Just pointy. Flat, Charlie thought, I'm going to have a flat, normal foot. Charlie laughed out loud as he slipped on his special shoe, the one made just to accommodate his foot. Soon he'd wear soft shoes and galoshes — the kind with buckles! — just like everyone else. It was a great day.

And then he remembered. Like a shot in the head. Jim Norton and the spy glass.

"Oh Jeeze, oh Jeeze." What could he do? What?

Charlie pulled on his other stocking and shoe, buttoned his shirt, and hip-hopped up the back stairs.

"Emma," Charlie hissed down the hall. "Emma."

"What is it you want?" Emma hollered back.

Right, the front bedroom.

"Emma, I need a favor." Charlie darted into the bedroom. Emma flung a sheet up into the air. It ballooned, and floated, before settling on the lumpy, horse-hair mattress. Charlie caught a corner of the bed sheet and made a feeble attempt to help make the bed.

"A favor? Let go of that." Emma cracked the sheet so hard it jerked out of Charlie's hand. "You've got more guts than a punt load of cod fish, Charlie Wilcox."

"I'll give you . . ." Charlie stopped. What did he have that the likes of Emma Fields would want? Money, that's what. "I'll give you a shilling if you go and get something for me."

"What?"

"First you have to say that you'll do it, and then you have to promise never to tell. You have to promise — cross your heart."

"I'll do no such thing. Tell me what it is first. And your shirt is buttoned up wrong."

Should he tell her? What if she went straight to Father and told him that he had taken the spy glass? It was a gamble. Charlie rebuttoned his shirt.

"It's up at Grave Hill. Jim . . ."

"Ready now, Charlie?" His father stood by the door.

Charlie panicked. Emma smiled. Whatever had Charlie all hot and bothered was just fine with her.

"I have to go see Jim," Charlie sputtered to Father, and Mother standing behind him, and Emma, too, since she was right there.

"Maybe we'll pass him on the road," said Lucy. She was in her Sunday best, a near-white summer skirt and blouse, snug at the waist, topped with a cream-colored long vest and black leather laced-up boots. She was a fine lookin' woman, that's what Father was always saying, "a fine lookin' woman."

"No, he's up Grave Hill. I have to see him."

"Charlie, we don't have time for that. And fix your shirt."

"No, but . . ." Charlie was desperate.

"No buts . . ."

"Oh here, let me," Lucy buttoned up Charlie's shirt.

In no time at all, Charlie, Lucy, and Skipper Sam set out down Harbor Drive to the train station. It wasn't more than ten minutes' walk, right through the village, and then up the path.

"Wait," Eliza Norton flew down her steps and out onto the road just as Mister Norton was drawing the carriage up to the gate.

"Whooo," Mister Norton stood tugging at the reins. The old nag clopped and stomped its feet, then finished the act with a sputter that sent horse spit all over the place.

"Such a disgusting animal," Eliza scowled at the beast. "Here, Charlie." She held out a box of cookies. "Take it, boy." Eliza's eyes watered up.

Lucy's mouth twitched. "Say thank you, Charlie."

"Thank you, Missus Eliza." Charlie reached for the cookies, using his solemn go-to-church face. He'd be a lot happier if he had a chance to talk to Jim.

"And here, I made you two a bite to eat on the train." Eliza held out a small wicker hamper.

"Oh, Eliza, thank you." Lucy took the hamper and hung it over her arm.

"My pleasure. Have you see my Jim? He'll want to see Charlie off." The adults looked up and down the road. Charlie stared steadily at his feet.

"Where could that boy be?" Eliza Norton shook her head and put her arm around Lucy. "I'll walk with you a bit, shall I? Or would you rather go by carriage?"

Lucy looked back at the sad pair, horse and driver, standing in the middle of the road.

"Let's walk." Which they did, down South and up to North Street.

"You take care now, Charlie," called Missus Lambe from the doorway of the butcher shop. "Have a good time in Montreal." And to Mister Lambe she said, "Doesn't he look happy."

"I'm not going to Montreal, Missus Lambe," Charlie hollered back. "I'm off to hospital to have my foot fixed."

"Oh dear, well have a good time anyway," Missus Lambe waved. And to Mister Lambe she said, "I thought he looked a little sad."

"Yes, my boy, just do what the nurses say," Mister Lambe chimed in. "Don't want them cutting off the wrong foot."

"Oh, James," Missus Lambe jabbed her husband in the stomach, not that he felt it, it being the size of a pumpkin and all.

"Oh, wait just a bit." Missus Lambe disappeared into the shop and reappeared with a bag of bull's-eyes and pepper-mint knobs mixed in. They weren't the usual fare for a butcher's shop, but Missus Lambe kept them on hand for sweet-tooth emergencies. "Don't eat them all at once now."

Charlie raced over and mumbled thanks.

He tried to pop a peppermint knob in his mouth, but couldn't. Not with the cookies in one hand and the bag in the other.

"Are you all going to the train station then?" Missus Lambe asked the little band. Without waiting for a reply she added, "Come now, Mister Lambe, close up shop. Let's walk our little Charlie to the station and see him off." So they did.

By now everyone in Brigus, least it seemed that way, had heard the news of Charlie going either to Montreal or to hospital. Either way, excitement was afoot. News came from Missus Pinkstone, who heard it from Missus Norton, who also passed it on to Missus Cozens, and the Browns.

"Hello, helloooo," crooned Missus Fox from across the road. She was all flushed and pink. "What's this, a pilgrimage?"

"Charlie's off to the hospital, Missus Fox." It was Missus Lambe who did the informing.

"Isn't that awful," Missus Fox said and then looked around at the smiling faces. "I mean, isn't that . . . wonderful?" Missus Lambe whispered the details into Missus Fox's good ear. Having nothing better to do, Missus Fox joined in the walk. So, too, came Missus Cozens and her two girls, Renee and Dulcie. Not to be left out, Mister Brown and his own father joined in. Everyone was talking and carrying on. It was a blooming parade.

Charlie strained his neck this way, then that. Jim was nowhere to be seen. Even Clint and Phil were missing. The thought was beginning to dawn on him that he was not going to get the spy glass down from Grave Hill. But he had to do something!

"Be brave," said Claire Guy, who popped up out of nowhere as usual. Charlie shrank at least a size.

"Hello, Claire," he mumbled.

"Here, Charlie." Claire handed him a bunch of dopey buttercups. "They're for you."

"Thanks." Now he had his bag, flowers, cookies, and candies to carry.

"Aren't you going to offer me a candy?"

Charlie rolled his eyes and handed over the bag. Claire took two, naturally.

What was he going to do about the spy glass? And then, an idea.

"Claire, I need you to find Jim," Charlie whispered.

"What for?" Claire was miffed. She was not going on a wild goose chase for nothing.

"Listen, Claire." Charlie moved as close to her as he dared and whispered as loud as he could. He fixed his eyes on his father's broad back. "Here, have another bull's-eye." Claire took two more. "I took, well, I mean I borrowed my father's spy glass. The one from the parlor, you know, the one brought over from England. It's up Grave Hill with Jim. Claire, you have to go and tell Jim to bring the glass back and put it in the parlor on the shelf . . ."

"Look, Charlie, there's Gwen. Bet she's wondering what you're saying to me," said Claire.

"Claire!" Charlie could have throttled her. "Claire, what am I saying to you?"

"Oh I don't know. Yoo-hoo." Claire gave Gwen a wave.

"CLAIRE!"

"And what do you two have your heads together about?" Claire's mother, Missus Guy, popped up between them and beamed, positively beamed. "Don't you two eat too many sweets now. You have your teeth to think about." Now that Charlie was going to have a regular foot he might turn out to be a catch for her Claire after all. Charlie was a Wilcox, don't forget.

Missus Fox interrupted with, "Missus Guy, I was lookin' out my window last night and didn't I see your Robert? It was past midnight! He looked to me like he was coming away from the Jubilee Club."

If there was trouble to be stirred up, you could be that sure Missus Fox was standing nearby with a spoon.

Missus Guy turned the color of cement.

"Not my Robert, Missus Fox . . ."

Missus Guy got busy defending the good character of her dear husband, who was known to take a drop. It was Charlie's last chance.

"Claire," Charlie hissed. "Go up to Grave Hill and tell . . ."

In the distance the train whistled, a long, thin, toneless howl.

"Here comes the Newfie Bullet, Charlie," more than one person hollered.

A brave amount of smoke belched out of the train's chimney as the black cone of the engine lurched into the station. The little band clambered up onto the wooden train platform.

"Say good-bye to everyone, Charlie." Sam threw his arm around Charlie's shoulder. Charlie felt little beside his father. And why not? He was a big man and a brave man — fair, too, was Skipper Sam. One of the best. "A better man as ever stood behind a pipe," was what people said. Charlie thought on that. What if Charlie just said, "Father, I took your spy glass. I'm sorry. It's up on Grave Hill. Jim Norton is guarding it. I'm really, really sorry." What could his father do? How mad could he get? Charlie opened his mouth.

"Charlie," Jim Norton leaped up and shouted. "Charlie, over here." Jim was at the back of the crowd.

"Jim," Charlie waved the half-dead buttercups in the air.

Charlie couldn't see him all that well. But he could sure see that Jim's hair was all stuck up and his shirt was rumpled, too.

"Off you go." Skipper Sam patted Charlie on the back and gave him a little nudge.

"Jim!" Charlie yelled back.

"Charlie!" Jim Norton kept bobbing up and down like a buoy in a storm.

A few byes, have an eye out, careful now, do what you are told. And slam. The door of the train compartment was shut. Steam hissed and gushed out from under the wheels of the train. It lurched back, forward, groaned, and then it was off. All hands were up in the air, waving this way and that, and away it went. The buttercups stuck in the door was all that could be seen as the train disappeared around the bend.

Chapter 4

*C*harlie sank like a stone into the train's red velvet coach seats. Lucy and Charlie had the whole train compartment to themselves, which would have been nice, had Charlie noticed. What was he going to do about the spy glass? He pushed aside the curtains and watched the land pass by. Rocks sprouted up here and there — as if they had been chucked down from heaven or coughed up from the earth.

"Here, Charlie, eat something." Lucy held out one of Missus Eliza's sandwiches. Charlie shook his head.

Lucy looked at her son. He was almost fourteen. Old enough to go to the ice fields as a cabin boy or, at the very least, a cookee. But Lucy couldn't bring herself to let him go to open sea, or even down to the Labrador. And Sam hadn't given her an argument. Odd that. Sam never talked about Charlie's foot, never treated him any different, at least not so as anyone could tell. But in this one thing, going to sea, Sam did not interfere with Lucy's decision. Most boys were on the boats by seven or so, down on the Labrador by nine or ten, and out on the ice by twelve. "He'll go when I'm ready to let him go, and that's that," Lucy had said to the Skipper some years back. No more was said from that day to this.

"Charlie, we have to talk. Doctors and nurses are very good people. But you must always do what you are told." Lucy spoke as if she was trying to convince herself, not Charlie. "And I'll visit every Sunday afternoon."

I have to tell her, thought Charlie. But maybe Jim will take the spy glass back on his own and sneak it into the house without anyone knowing.

"Now, I've sewn a dollar into your trousers. Your Aunt Maude lives on Circular Road in St. John's. In a pinch she'll set you straight."

If he was to tell her, now would be the time. With everything quiet like.

"About the operation. I don't know all the details, the doctor knows best, but your foot, Charlie, it will be better. I mean it will be flat to walk on, but it won't be perfect. It's to do with your tendon, a muscle. They will sort of shorten it, or lengthen it, or something."

He'd just say, Mother, I took Father's spy glass. No, that sounded like he lost it. Mother, I borrowed Father's spy glass. Better.

"Did I tell you I'll come to visit every Sunday? I don't want you to be afraid, Charlie."

Mother, the spy glass was just lying there and I thought

it best that it was used. That sounded sensible. And his mother was always saying, "Be sensible."

"Now, you have seven pairs of clean underwear."

Mind, the glass could be back where it belonged at this very moment. But what was Jim going on about at the station? Maybe Clint found them out. No, no sense thinking like that. Drive him mental, that would.

"Oh, Charlie, you're so quiet." Lucy twisted a hankie between her fingers.

And then a thought. He'd tell her at the hospital. Yes, that's it. At the hospital door. He'd whisper it into her ear. "Mother," he'd say, "Jim Norton has something to tell you." Charlie perked right up.

ONCE OFF THE TRAIN, Lucy and Charlie took the streetcar directly to St. John's General Hospital. It was a fine city, St. John's. Big, very big, and busy, too. Oh sure, some said it was a filthy place, all sooty and grim, and teaming with poverty, but Charlie took no notice. It was exciting. Lots of shops and electric cars and people walking quickly. Charlie pressed his nose against the window of the streetcar. When he grew up he'd live here, for a while anyway. He'd be a city boy then, not a bayman all his life.

"Here we are." Lucy stood up, one hand clutching the overhead strap to steady herself, the other reaching for Charlie's bag.

Lucy stomped off the streetcar, looking neither right nor left. A lady wearing the biggest straw hat, secured to her head by a frightening hat pin as long as his arm, plowed into Charlie. She never even said "excuse me."

Charlie tried to keep up to his mother. A boy on the corner, dressed in knickers and a wool cap, held up the pink *Evening Telegram* and hollered, "War escalates in Europe."

War?

"Mother," Charlie ran up beside his mom. "Did ya hear that — about the war?"

Of course they heard about the war in Brigus. Some days it was all anyone talked about. But to see the word — *war* — written like that, it seemed real all of a sudden.

"Never you mind. It has nothing to do with us. There," she pointed to a building that squatted like a gray stone monster on top of the hill. Near took Lucy Wilcox's breath away.

"Come along, Charlie." Lucy hiked her skirt and stormed the hill like the enemy army was at her back. Charlie scrambled behind her, matching two steps to his mother's one.

The decision was made, the moment of truth had arrived. Charlie would tell her about the spy glass right now! "Mother . . ."

His mother stood in front of the great doors. With one swift tug, Lucy swung them open.

"Mother."

"Wait here, Charlie, I'll just see that all the papers are in order." Lucy trundled off down the hall, all business, her shoes click-clacking on the wooden floors. Like she knew where she was going, like she had been there before.

Charlie plunked himself on a hard wooden bench to wait. No one took much notice of him. Seemed to Charlie that no one took much notice of each other either. Still, it didn't look like a bad place. And then his mom was back again, with a lady dressed in white beside her.

"Charlie, please stand up and meet Miss Northwood."

Two cold eyes glared down at Charlie. Miss Northwood, head nurse, in the whitest, stiffest clothes imaginable, was the most terrifying woman Charlie Wilcox had ever laid eyes on.

"Charlie, say hello please."

Charlie just stared.

"Charlie!" Lucy looked distraught.

"Well, Charles, we won't waste any more time will we? Let's get you to your bed. Say good-bye to your mother," said Miss Northwood.

"Mother, can I talk to you?" asked Charlie.

"None of that, Charles," Miss Northwood interjected. "Just say your good-byes. We don't want any nonsense. You're too big for nonsense." Miss Northwood reached out and grabbed at Charlie's hand. He snapped it back.

"Mother . . ." Charlie pleaded.

The hand descended on his shoulder. It pinched.

"Good-bye, Missus Wilcox. We can manage from here," said Miss Northwood.

"No, Mother I just want to . . ." Charlie squirmed out of Miss Northwood's reach.

"Charlie . . ." Lucy was at a loss.

"That will be all, Missus Wilcox." Lucy Wilcox was dismissed. All of that conviction that helped Lucy stomp up the hill and charge into the hospital vanished. Tears brimmed in her eyes. She couldn't speak, not a word.

"Mother, Mother," Charlie was near yelling. One hand

on his shoulder became two and now he was doubly trapped. Lucy turned and walked, faster, then ran down the hall and through the doors.

"MOTHER! I have to say something."

"Come on, boy."

"I just want to tell her something." He glared up at his captor.

"Come along," Miss Northwood glared back. "I've dealt with the likes of you many times, and you might as well know it now, young man — this is a hospital and we don't tolerate nonsense here."

Charlie shook himself loose and made a break.

"I just want to tell my mother something. I have to." He yelled over his shoulder and ran, hip-hop, down the corridor.

"Stop him." Miss Northwood's command reverberated off the walls. Two beefy male orderlies jumped in front of the door. Charlie skidded, tripped, and hit the floor like a wet mop.

The orderlies dragged their prisoner back down the hall and stopped short in front of Miss Northwood.

"Well, I never. Take him up to Ward 3. And there," Miss Northwood pointed to Charlie's bag, box of cookies, and bag of sweets, "are his belongings. He is in Nurse Butters' ward. As for you, Charles Wilcox, I hope you will have composed yourself before you get there." Miss Northwood spun on her heels and marched off.

And so Charlie, silent and angry, was escorted down the corridor and dropped like a parcel in front of a nursing station.

"He's all yours," said one of the orderlies to Nurse Butters, ward nurse.

Nurse Butters muttered something but didn't look up from her papers.

Charlie bit back tears. What was wrong with his mother? Why had she left him like that? All he wanted to do was tell her about the spy glass. But she just ran away!

"So, Charles Wilcox." Nurse Butters looked up to give him a quick once-over. "Just wait here. Nurse will give you a bath before getting you into bed."

"It's Charlie and I had a bath today." It was hard to speak and choke back tears at the same time.

Nurse Butters was not impressed. "All patients must have a bath and be checked for lice and crabs." Charlie's head snapped up. Lice? Crabs?

"I don't have them," hissed Charlie. Where'd she think he came from? Didn't she know that he was a Wilcox?

"What is that?" Nurse Butters pointed to his bag of sweets and box of cookies.

"Cookies and candies," said Charlie.

"No food on the ward. Leave it here."

"But . . ."

"Here." Nurse Butters tapped her finger on the desk.

Charlie did as he was told. What else could he do?

"Just stand by the window and stay out of the way." Nurse Butters went back to her paperwork.

A thin breeze blew in through the white bars of the window. Just like a prison, thought Charlie. He looked out. In the distance was the sea — the same sea he looked on every single day of his life. But it looked different from here, unreachable, foreign. And then the city, a mishmash of buildings, clapboard mostly but some stone, too. And below him gardens, bushes all clumped together, ratty old plants that didn't flower too much.

And then he saw her, way, way over there. Sitting, just sitting on a bench, her straw hat beside her, head bent down, an arm holding it up. Bits of hair had come loose from the bun in the back. They swung in front of her face, swaying softly like a light wind was pushing them. And her shoulders were heaving, up and down. She was crying. Crying.

"MOTHER." Charlie put two hands on the bars and stuck his head out as far as it would go. "MOTHER."

The ward came alive just like a beehive struck with a stick. Instantly. Patients called out. Nurses ran. A tray hit the floor.

"Stop it. Stop it this instant." Nurse Butters swooped down on him like some big, mean white bird. She reached over, pulled his head in, ouch, his ears near came off, and slammed the windows shut.

"How dare you. We have sick people here." Nurse Butters, who wasn't old or young, pretty or ugly, was plain livid. With a twist of her wrist she locked the window and scurried over to some fellow who was having trouble breathing. Charlie collapsed against the wall.

"Hey, bayman, miss your mommy?" A nasty-looking kid with a head like a potato, pig eyes, and a pig nose stuck in the middle, stood behind a counter not five feet from Charlie.

Charlie said not a word, just hung his head.

"Ah, the little sissy is a crybaby."

It was as if Charlie's arm wasn't even attached to his body because, without his say-so, Charlie took a giant step forward and popped the kid in the face. Just like that, one of the best punches Charlie had ever thrown. The kid didn't even have time to duck. Just stood there, bang, got it right in the mouth. He toppled like an egg and crashed to the floor.

Charlie moved around the counter, fists ready.

"Get up," he cried. "Come on, get up." And then a scream. But it didn't come from the kid either, it came from Charlie himself. Charlie's head swiveled back to the counter, back again to the kid on the floor, and back to the counter — like he couldn't take it in. And then he understood. The kid hadn't been standing *behind* the counter, he'd been sitting *on* the counter.

The boy lay on the ground, dazed. He wouldn't be getting up on his own, not likely.

He had no legs.

"I hit a cripple." Charlie sunk slowly to the floor, put his head in his hands, and sobbed.

Chapter 5

Nurse Mac (her real name was Nurse MacKenzie) was efficient about it. "Lift," she said, nicely though, as nicely as you can when collecting pisspots from under bums.

Charlie hated it. "Why can't I go to the toilet on me own?" This made no sense. He lay in this ivory-painted, cast-iron bed from morn to night and then morn again, doing nothing, as if he was sick, which he wasn't, not a t'all.

"It's the rules, Charlie, you know that," said Mac.

"There's more rules here than there are people," Charlie snapped back.

"Now, Charlie, be a good boy." Mac was nice, really nice. He liked her blonde hair and the way it kept getting loose from her cap. Her eyes were nice — blue eyes that crinkled up in the corners. She smiled nicely, too. And her hands were always warm, not like Nurse Butters'. She had hands as cold as a fresh cod.

"Tell you what, I'll see if I can't get an extra dessert for you tonight. And you, too, Davy. How about it?"

Davy shrugged. Mac smiled gently, like she always did, before going on her way.

"Your turn, Charlie." Davy slapped down a queen.

Davy might not have had any legs but he was good at cards. Had to be, so he said, nothing else to do except maybe scribble and draw pictures. He did that a lot but nothing Charlie was allowed to look at.

Davy's teeth crunched down on something.

"What ya eating?" Charlie asked.

"Candy."

"Oh, give me one. They took mine away. What do you have?"

Davy rolled over and pulled a brown bag out from under his bedclothes.

"Bull's-eyes and peppermint knobs."

"What? Hey, they're mine!" Charlie was indignant.

"In that case you can have one." Davy flicked over a peppermint knob. "Consider it payment." Davy pointed to his black eye, which wasn't all that black. "Now put down a card."

Charlie slapped down a ten of hearts.

"How'd you hurt your legs?" Charlie asked, tentatively.

"Hurt my legs? What, you think I hurt my own legs?" Davy snarled. "Think I took an ax to them? Think I just chopped 'em off 'cause I didn't like the look of them? Your turn."

Two years had passed since a streetcar lopped off Davy's legs. Two years of people asking him dumb questions. He was bored with the questions. The only thing worse would be if people stopped asking questions.

"And don't ask how I lost 'em, either," Davy carried on. "People say to me, 'So how did you lose your legs?' Like my legs were umbrellas and I left them on a streetcar. I didn't leave them *on* a streetcar, I left them *under* a streetcar. And I didn't do it 'cause I was forgetful, either. I never looked down one day and said, 'Oh look, my legs is missing, where'd I leave 'em?'" He tossed down his last card. "You lose."

Davy was the only other kid in a ward of men. His bed was parked beside Charlie's. A tin chest of drawers on loppy wheels was between them, and sometimes a tissue-thin cotton curtain, too. It was near see-through.

On his first full day in hospital, Charlie saw the shadow of legs without the bottom halves, through the curtain, when the doctor examined Davy's stumps. The legs had been cut off just under each knee, one stump being a little longer than the other.

"Did it hurt?" Charlie just had to ask.

Davy shuffled and dealt the cards out again. "Ya mean when my legs were cut off?"

Charlie nodded and waited for the blast of Davy's wrath. Didn't come though.

"Don't think so. Don't remember. I was running across the tracks with me pal. I fell and then I woke up here. I don't even hardly remember the streetcar coming at me.

It hurt later, days and weeks later. But naw, can't recall it hurting at the time."

"What was it like?"

"You're a Nosey Parker. I told ya, I fell and next thing I knows I was looking at my legs and one was gone. They had to chop off the other one here in the hospital. Saved me knees though."

"Is that good?"

"Sure it's good. Only problem is — sometimes my feet itch."

Charlie's mouth gaped open. "But they're gone!"

"You're a bright boy. Bet nobody can fool you. Play."

Charlie tossed down a jack and flopped back onto his pillow.

"Your mouth's open. Shut it." Davy slapped down a king.

"Sorry. So what do ya do?" Charlie leaned out of his bed and across the gulf of space.

"About what?"

"The itch."

"I scratch it." Davy slapped down another king. "You lose, again."

THAT NIGHT, after the nurse had inspected the patients, after the lights were switched off, Charlie had a dream. He saw his dad floating out to sea on a raft. Charlie tried to reach him. His arms stretched and stretched until they turned into floppy rubber. He couldn't reach his dad no matter how hard he tried.

THERE WERE NO contagious diseases on this ward. Some were in to have their insides tampered with — a gall-bladder operation, or something to come out, like tonsils. But mostly they were men all lined up in metal beds with bits missing off of them. Accidents mostly, but some had lost their feet, legs, hands, arms, or fingers in the cold, seal-ing, maybe, or fishing.

Three days a week all the patients that could be moved were shunted down to the solarium. It was sunny and warm in there, with lots of hanging plants that dusted the top of your head if you weren't careful. Charlie was allowed to walk to the solarium, but only if Nurse Butters wasn't about. Davy was taken off somewheres, Charlie didn't know where. In the warm sunlight and flower-filled air, Charlie played checkers or drafts with Ol' Tom. He had one leg gone bad and an arm off.

"It's not that I mind losing the arm, boy," said Ol' Tom in a near whisper. "It's me hand. Man ain't worth much with-out two hands."

There was plenty of talk about the war. "The Huns will get it now," Ol' Tom said. Charlie didn't know what a Hun was but Ol' Tom sure did. "Cruelest, meanest bloody beg-gars ever to walk upright," he said, while nodding his head vigorously. He was agreeing with himself.

"Be over and done with soon, I expect," said Watson, a small man with sad eyes. Watson, older than Ol' Tom, with a bad back that caused him to cry out in pain now and then, had fought in the Boer War. He knew about war.

Mostly Charlie sat beside Ol' Tom and stared out the window and watched the ships coming and going in the harbor.

"They be taking on hands," said Ol' Tom. "Maybe need a cabin boy or cookee, hey?" He gave Charlie a wink.

Nine days had passed since Charlie's mother had dropped him off at the hospital door. She had brought him new underwear once, not that he needed it, dressed like he was in a dumb shift that didn't even cover his behind up proper. They hardly spoke at all. His mom looked awful sad and then the nurse said she had to go. It wasn't a proper visit at all.

Nine long, boring, lonely days. He was tired a lot. Tired of doing nothing.

Charlie hadn't mentioned the spy glass to his mother. He thought of writing a letter to Jim and asking about it, but letters were not personal sorts of things in Brigus. They were events. Why, if a letter arrived in the house it would be read out at breakfast and then passed from person to person down the table, over the brewis and mugs of steaming tea. Besides, what could he say? He was a coward and a thief. He had taken something that was important and now it might be lost. Anyways, what would he tell them about this place? Maybe he was in St. John's, only an hour and a bit away by train, but it felt like he could have been on another continent.

"Charlie, you asleep?" Davy was always whispering to Charlie just as he was drifting off.

"Not anymore."

"The doctor came by today."

No news. The doctor always came by. He didn't actually do anything but he came by anyway.

"Charlie, you hear me?"

"Yea."

"The doctor told me something today." Davy leaned so far out of bed that Charlie thought he might take a tumble.

"Not so loud." If they were caught talking again after lights out, they'd be in for it good.

"What did the doctor say?" At the best of times Davy was irritating. At 1:00 a.m. he was plain annoying.

"He said that I was going to die."

THE CLATTER OF THE breakfast trays woke him. Charlie sat up way too fast and stared at Davy's empty bed.

"Up," Mac stood at the foot of his bed. "Time to change your bedclothes."

"Where's Davy?" He scanned the ward.

"Come on. Up you get." Charlie hopped out of bed and stood waiting, bare bum to the wind. In broad strokes Mac whipped off the sheets. His top sheet became his bottom sheet and the old bottom sheet, which had already had both sides slept on, was rolled into a lump.

"Mac, where is Davy?" Charlie was now frantic.

"He's off to have his bath. There now, your bed is fresh and clean." Mac patted the bed. Charlie hopped back in.

"So — he's not dead?"

"Dead?" Mac was genuinely shocked.

"No, I just wondered. He wasn't here when I woke up."

"I think you need fresh air, Charlie Wilcox." Mac ruffled his hair and tucked him in. She seemed uneasy, uncomfortable like.

"Mac, where are Davy's parents?"

"Davy is a ward of the courts, Charlie. His mother could not afford the hospital bills."

"Where's his father?"

"Mind your p's & q's, you Nosey Parker. Don't you worry about Davy. He won't be with us much longer."

"MacKenzie, come to the nurse's station immediately." Nurse Butters appeared out of nowhere and barked out her command. Even Charlie jumped.

"Yes, ma'am. Quick, Charlie, get into bed." Mac suddenly looked pale.

"What do you mean — he won't be with us much longer?" whispered Charlie.

"I can't talk now. Just be a good boy. And, Charlie, I have a secret for you. See down there?" Mac pointed to the tin drawer that separated the beds. "There's a box of sweets from your mother." As she was about to dash, Mac turned and said, "You know the rules, no food on the wards so be careful." Mac was off, fast and silent. She went past all the beds and into Nurse Butters' glass office. Davy called the office the guard's post. There was another man in there, old Dr. McKnight.

Davy was wheeled back by the same barrel-shaped orderly who carted Charlie up to the floor twelve days gone.

"Where've you been? I thought you were dead." Charlie bolted upright and crossed his arms.

"Disappointed?" Davy grinned. The orderly dropped Davy on the bed. Just like that. Plop. "Thank you, my good man." Davy dismissed the orderly with a flick of the wrist. "Jeeze, what a chump."

"Are ya really dying?"

"Oh I am, but not yet, I mean, not today."

"When?"

"Soon, very soon. Maybe in a week."

"You look fine."

Davy raised his hand to his brow. "Oh, I look better than I am. But who knows when it will happen? Maybe I'll just go to sleep tonight and wake up dead."

"What are you dying of?" asked Charlie.

"Hyperscholocilous halitosis."

"What's that?"

"A fatal disease. Now stop bothering me. I need my rest." Davy got annoyed easy.

"Then how come they won't let your mother and father come see you?"

Instantly Charlie knew that he had crossed the line.

"Don't ya know, they don't allow visitors. Now leave me alone." He spat out the words and turned his head.

"Davy . . ." Charlie flopped back on his pillow. He didn't mean any harm. That was the problem with words — once you said them, you couldn't unsay them.

And then Charlie had a thought. "Davy, is something wrong with Mac?"

"She's in love. Leave me alone."

"In love?" He wasn't sure, but there had to be a rule against that.

"Yea, Dr. Robert Daniels. He's on another floor. I've seen him."

Nurse Mac in love. Charlie's stomach took a tumble.

"Will she get sacked?"

"Probably. If they find out."

"I think somebody already knows. Look." Charlie pointed down the row of beds to the glass office. They could see Mac standing in front of Nurse Butters' desk. Her head

was bowed and she was shaking it from side to side.
Dr. McKnight stood off to one side.

Davy gave a low whistle. "Well, that's it then. She's a
goner."

Chapter 6

"Well, young man, the big day is tomorrow." Dr. McKnight made the announcement while standing at the foot of Charlie's bed.

"Tomorrow?" Charlie near leapt for joy.

"You'll be operated on at 9:00 in the morning." And away he went. White coat flapping, heels clicking. No explanation, no words of encouragement, nothing.

Mac stood beside his bed. Her eyes were puffy and rimmed with red.

"Mac, what's wrong? Aren't you happy for me?"

"Oh, Charlie, of course I'm happy for you, darling. Everything will go fine. You'll see." Mac tucked his sheet in too tight.

"Mac, were you crying?" Charlie asked again.

"Good heavens, no," Mac's mouth smiled, but her eyes didn't. "Your lunch is coming soon. Eat it all up. You'll not be getting much food after that." Mac walked away so fast she was near running.

"Something is wrong with Mac," Charlie whispered to Davy. "Do you think she got the sack?"

"Who cares. She's got two legs, hasn't she? Her life can't be that bad." Davy was in a foul mood.

"What's wrong with you?"

"Let me tell you." That's how Davy was — if you asked, he answered. Then he stopped and his voice changed, becoming softer. "Charlie, what do you think about death?"

"Not much," answered Charlie.

"Well, what I'm asking is, do you think cowards go to hell or purgatory?"

"That would depend." Charlie squirmed in his bed.

"On what?" asked Davy.

"On what the coward did." Charlie didn't like where this conversation was going.

"Well, what I was thinking was, what if they operated on your other foot? You know, by accident." Davy plastered an inquisitive look on his face.

"No, they won't." Charlie felt ill.

"Oh yea? What about the guy that was in your very bed afore you? Came in to have a finger off and they took off his whole hand. They did! And it was the wrong hand, too. And see that guy over there," he pointed down the long row of beds to a patient swathed in bandages. He looked like a mummy. "Near amputated his ears. And," said Davy, as he leaned over the great divide between the two beds, "he came in to the hospital with — a stomachache!" Davy was triumphant.

Charlie's own stomach heaved. He went white with fear.

"Charlie," Davy whispered across the divide, "Charlie, let's escape."

"Escape?"

"Yea, tonight. Just for a few hours. You're not being operated on until tomorrow. And who knows what might happen after that. Maybe you'll be dead. Here you are, your life hangin' by a thread over an open grave, and now you have a chance for one last adventure!" Davy was on a roll. "Think on it, Charlie, maybe this is your last night on earth. Come on. Don't be a coward."

The word *coward* stung.

"You're crazy." Charlie turned his back on Davy.

"I thought you said that you were sorry. I thought you felt bad — you know, about leaving me, and about me dying. I thought — since this may be your last night — you may want to see the stars. Just one more time." Davy said the last bit slowly, like a bad actor.

"Well, I do but . . ." Charlie was at a loss.

"All I want to do is get outside and see the stars. Is that too much to ask? Come on, Charlie."

Ridiculous. How could they get outside without being seen? Wheelchairs were huge, besides they squeaked something terrible. And he couldn't carry Davy. But what if Davy was really dying. What if he died too?

"How?"

"I've got a plan."

"YOU AWAKE?"

"Yea," Charlie whispered as loud as he dared. He stretched his legs and feet, and wiggled his twisted one. It wouldn't be long now. And then a thought — what if he was caught? What if, as punishment, he couldn't have the operation?

"Davy," Charlie hissed.

"Charlie, is that you?" Nurse Mac stopped at the foot of Charlie's bed. "It's almost midnight. Can't you sleep?" Mac didn't wait for an answer. She came round to the side of his bed and brushed his hair with her hand. "I'm on double-duty. I'll be here when you come out of the operation. There's nothing to be afraid of, now go to sleep."

"Mac?" Charlie whispered as she was about to turn away. "Is everything all right?"

"You'll be fine, Charlie."

"No, I mean about you?"

"Oh, Charlie, don't worry about me. Sleep now."

Mac pivoted on her heels and faded into the shadows.

"Jeeze, what are you starting a conversation for? We got ta move if we're going to make it."

"Davy, I don't think we should do this."

"You're a right little coward, Charlie Wilcox."

"Boys, quiet down there." It was Ol' Tom's voice, or maybe it was the new man, Percy somebody.

Charlie threw himself back on his pillow and stared at the dark ceiling.

"Move, it's time," commanded Davy.

With a monumental effort Charlie sat up and tossed off his covers. First, the clothes. They weren't going to go far with their bums hanging out. Charlie crawled out of bed, plumped the pillows, tossed a cover over the lot, and skulked around the beds to the lockers by the far wall. He grabbed what he could and headed back.

"Pass 'em," Davy hissed through the dark. Charlie tossed over Davy's sweater and pants. Davy pulled the sweater over his head, yanked on his pants, and pinned up both legs.

"Know what they say about a guy who has both his feet planted firmly on the ground?" Davy whispered through the half-light.

"Quiet." Charlie snapped back.

"They say that he can't get his pants on." Davy cackled. "Can't say that about me!"

"This is no time for dumb jokes." Charlie's heart thumped so loud he thought it might wake up the whole ward.

"You have no sense of humor."

"I have no sense." Charlie pulled up his pants.

"Don't go chickening out on me, Wilcox."

Charlie, his nightgown tucked into his pants and a sweater on top, hip-hopped over to Davy's bed.

"You ready?"

Davy nodded.

Charlie put both arms under Davy's armpits and lowered him to the floor.

"Ouch. Oh, ouch. Careful."

"You're heavy." But Davy wasn't all that heavy. Funny, thought Charlie, legs must weigh a lot.

The nursing shift was changing over and all the nurses were crowding in Nurse Butters' office to get their instructions. The hallway to freedom ran right past this same office. How would the two of them slip by without being noticed? Charlie thought this was a problem. Davy didn't seem to pay it any mind.

"Do the beds look all right?" whispered Charlie.

Davy strained to look over Charlie's handiwork. The pillows looked human enough — if you didn't look too close. Davy nodded.

"You go first," said Davy.

Charlie started out. It wasn't safe to crawl between the rows; they'd have to crawl under the beds. A bald, mean light shone out from Nurse Butters' office. It cast long, thin shadows that ended in sharp points. Charlie made it under three, four beds and then, a rattling noise followed by a *ker-chunk, splash, bonk.*

Charlie moaned.

"What?" growled Davy.

"I spilled a pisspot," Charlie whispered back.

"Go around."

"It's disgusting."

"Keep going."

Charlie stopped at the last bed, old Christopher Adams' — he could tell by the snore. Charlie was so close to Nurse Butters' office he could hear the old crow talking. Davy crawled up beside him.

"Ready?"

Charlie nodded. Well, he certainly didn't want to go back to that mess under the bed. "Are you sure it's there?"

"I've been here for a long time," hissed Davy. "Sure I'm sure."

The hall, or rather freedom, was directly ahead.

"Go, go." Davy motioned Charlie on.

Charlie wiggled forward, stood, and lurched ahead, ducking first under the window of the office and then rolling under a gurney. Made it. He was in the dimly lit hallway. It was deathly quiet, spooky really. Not a nurse in sight. He turned back. Now, where was it? Yes, there, just as Davy said. Parked by the door was an empty, floor-washing tub on four lopsided wheels. A mop handle stuck out the back.

Charlie gave Davy the nod. Davy's eyes flickered under the bed like a cat's, then he made a break. He wiggled his body this way and that. A snake could do no better. And then — a door opened. Footsteps. Charlie near stopped breathing altogether. Davy rolled behind a set of drawers and waited. The door closed and the footsteps faded.

Again Davy wiggled and, inch by inch, he made his way toward Charlie. His bare arms made squeaking sounds on the floor, and Charlie could hear him huffing and puffing. With one gigantic push, Davy heaved himself into the hall.

"Quick, help me into the bucket. We don't have much time left. The nurses will be out any second."

Davy's reasoning went like this: the nurses would be holed up in their meeting about the midnight shift change for another two, maybe three minutes. Meeting or no, they'd hear a squeaky wheelchair being pushed down the hall. But who would notice the sound of a cleaner's tub rattling about? Thing was, people took no mind of cleaners, their buckets, or the noise they made.

The two spoke not a word. Charlie took hold of Davy, lifted him up, and plopped him in the bucket. He fit, just. Charlie grabbed the mop handle and gave the whole rig a mighty shove. They were off.

"Push hard and be as loud as you want," Davy hissed to Charlie.

Down the hall they went, then up a small ramp to the floor above.

"Faster," said Davy.

"I'm going as fast as I can." The washing bucket kept veering off to one side, then the other. Davy was right, no one took any notice. A doctor came out of a doorway ahead of them. Davy and Charlie near froze in their tracks but he never even turned around.

Another floor, another ramp. Up they went.

"Stop." Davy commanded. "There's no one on this floor at night."

Breathless, Charlie pushed the rig off into the shadows, slumped against the wall, and closed his eyes. His heart was thumping so loud it hurt his eardrums.

"Charlie!" Davy screamed.

"Jeeze!"

The tub, and Davy too, was off. Down a ramp he sailed.

"Charlie!" Davy screamed again.

"Oh, Jeeze, Davy." Charlie gave chase.

Davy hit two swinging doors and disappeared.

Then Charlie heard it. Smack, the sound of a dead fish landing on newspaper. Crack, the sound of a stick being snapped in half.

Charlie came flying through the doors and stopped in his tracks. He stared down at the carnage. The bucket was belly up, its wheels spinning in the air. Davy lay belly up too.

"Davy, speak to me." Charlie knelt beside the body. "Davy, say something."

"How could you not see the down ramp? Are you blind and stupid?"

He was alive. "I hate you, Charlie Wilcox."

Ah, Davy was his old self, although slightly damaged.

"Anything broke?"

"Quiet, listen."

The two perked up their ears and listened for sounds of danger.

Nothing. The hall was empty.

"Help me up," said Davy.

"Are you sure?"

"No, I'm not sure. Just get me back into the bucket."

Charlie put the bucket right side up and wrapped his arms around Davy's waist to hoist him up. It was then that he spotted an old wheelchair off in the shadows.

"Look," Charlie pointed. Whoops, Davy slipped out of Charlie's grasp. He thumped back down on the floor. "Oh, Davy, I'm sorry."

Again Davy lay flapping on the floor like a beached carp. If he could, he would have punched Charlie's lights out right there and then.

"Are you trying to murder me?" Davy muttered.

"Oh, sorry. Oh, Davy, really, I'm really . . . you all right?"

"No, I'm not all right. I'm half-killed. Pull that wheelchair over here and stay away from me."

Charlie hip-hopped over to the chair and pushed it alongside Davy.

"Here, let me . . ."

"Get away from me. You're a jinker," snarled Davy.

With a heave, Davy swung himself into the chair. "All right, we haven't much farther to go. Just down this hall, around the corner, and there's the door to the roof."

"Here, let me push." It was the least Charlie could do.

"Don't you dare. Get away!" Davy put his palms on the wheels and gave them a shove.

Sure enough, the door leading to the roof was right where Davy said it was. Charlie grabbed hold of the door handle and swung the door open. It creaked something terrible.

"Oh, no," said Charlie.

"What? What's wrong?" Davy followed Charlie's gaze. The two stared into a dark, gaping hole. Steps, dozens and dozens of them. Rock ones, too. Old, craggy, chipped stone steps that curled up and away and were lost in the dark.

"Davy, did you know about the steps?"

"I knew where the door was, didn't I? I just never opened it before. Couldn't expect to know everything." Davy's lip quivered. "Well, I'll just go up arse first."

"Davy, even if you could get up, you'd never get back down."

"Always the quitter, aren't you? Well, sometimes ya just gotta do what's right. Maybe it's not right for you, but it's right for me, now get out of my way. I'm going outside this night." Davy twisted his body in the chair and began to lower himself down to the ground.

"Wait," said Charlie. "There's no sense going all the way up if the door at the top is locked. Just stay here."

Charlie plunged into the dark and began the circular climb.

Past the first curve it was pitch black. Charlie felt the damp and clammy stone walls on either side with his hands as he climbed. Finally he felt wood. The door. The handle. A turn, a kick, and moon and starlight filled the tiny space. Davy was right, after all.

"Davy, Davy, can you hear me?" Charlie bellowed down the spiral tunnel.

"Yea, and so can the whole hospital."

"Davy, you are right."

Charlie stumbled out onto the roof of the hospital. The night was so clear you could near touch it. And the moon — he could almost read by it. And over there you could see the great city of St. John's herself, the wharf and the sea and all. Hear it, too, if you strained. Charlie gulped down fresh air and stumbled around the funnels and chimneys before turning back to the door. He hollered down the steps. "Davy?"

"Put a cork in it." Davy was at the first crook of the stairs. Up he came, sliding on his bum, grunting and taking each breath like it was his last.

"Can I help?" offered Charlie.

"Would you get it through your head. You are no help. You are a menace. Leave me be."

It took awhile. Finally Davy reached the top, and, mustering every bit of strength, he threw his whole body out the door and onto the roof.

Charlie clapped his hands and bounced about. "You did it, you did it."

"'Course I did it," Davy cracked a smile.

"Look, over here." Charlie found a couple of old rugs. "Looks like we aren't the first to escape to the roof." He made two soft seats against a chimney. "How'd you find out about this place?"

"I heard some of the orderlies talking about it," said Davy. "I just asked one of them how to get up here, that's all."

The stars above them looked like pinpricks in the sky, little holes, like if you looked through them you could see heaven itself.

"'Star so light, star so bright . . .'" Charlie whispered.

"You are a right baby, aren't you?"

"What, you never make wishes?"

"Well, for starters, there's more than one star up there." Davy was smug.

"So? 'Stars so light, stars so bright.'"

"What?" smirked Davy. "You going to make a thousand wishes?"

"No." said Charlie. "Just one."

"One wish? Maybe I'll make one wish too. Humm. What would I wish for? New legs maybe. OK, let's see, 'Stars so light, stars so bright, all the stars I see tonight, I wish I may, I wish I might . . . get a pair of new legs.' There, let's see if my wish comes true."

There was nothing to say after that. The two sat in silence and watched the night.

"I'm sorry, Davy."

"What's to be sorry about?"

Charlie shrugged.

"Look here," said Davy. "I've seen dozens of you sissies come and go over the last two years. So you are going to get a new foot, so what? Think that's going to solve all your problems? That's how everybody thinks. If they just get a berth, if they make more money, if they just get a this or a that, then everything will be perfect. Well, it won't. Besides, I'm dying, so it doesn't matter."

"Quiet." Charlie bolted upright. "Listen."

A door opened somewhere, not the same door they

came up but another door, off in the distance. And then footsteps.

"Do you see anyone?"

Charlie shook his head. There was a clinking sound, then a knock and the sound of a match being struck against brick. The thin point of light glowed from a pipe. "It's a man," whispered Charlie. It was an easy deduction, since women did not smoke pipes, least no women Charlie ever met.

The door opened again, more footsteps, these ones lighter than the last, and quicker.

"Who is it?"

"Shut up. I can't tell."

"Let's get closer."

The two boys inched toward the flicker of light, stopping short behind a series of tin chimneys.

"How come they're not talking?" whispered Davy from behind.

"I don't . . ." and then Charlie knew why they weren't talking.

And Davy did, too. He swallowed a great "whoop!"

"They're kissing," Charlie smothered his laugh with his hand.

"Be quiet. Listen."

The words of the strangers wafted across the roof.

"I'll have to leave or I'll be let go in disgrace."

"You can stay at my mother's. It won't be for long."

"I hardly think that would work, Robert. A lady like your mother! I'm sure she'd love to have an outcast, an orphan at that, on her doorstep."

"Mother's not like that."

"Robert, I've made my own way since I was fourteen years old. I'll be fine. I'm very resourceful."

"Davy, Davy, it's Mac!" Charlie's heart near leaped out of his mouth. He wanted to yell, except no words came out.

"I'll go to Dr. McKnight and explain," said the male voice.

"Well, I know who that is," whispered Davy. "That's Dr. Robert Daniels. I told you Mac was in love. Didn't I tell you? Didn't I?"

Charlie ground his fingers into the wall. He wanted to do something, anything, just to make it all stop.

"What do you know. Mac and Daniels. I was right," chuckled Davy. "This is great!"

"Robert, it won't do any good, you'll be let go, too. It's all such a shame. But it doesn't matter now. Butters has found us out. I am to report to Northwood tomorrow and that will be that. It won't really change our plans, now will it? It's just a shame to leave like this."

"The old fool," muttered Robert.

Mac let out a deep, long sigh. "Butters and McKnight — did you ever meet two people more alike? You know I heard that many, many years ago they were almost married."

"I couldn't see those two dried-up old cods as anything more than what they are now."

"Oh, Robert, don't say that, they're only following rules."

"Rules, what good are rules if they only hurt people? I work twelve hours a day, so do you. We both love medicine, and if we fall in love, we are canned. And, Lily, I do love you."

"Oh, Robert."

"I'm going to be sick." Davy made a face.

"I didn't know her name was Lily," Charlie said softly.

"We must report tomorrow afternoon. I have a fitting, of course." Robert paused. "Did you hear something?"

"No, nothing," said Mac.

"Quiet." Robert whispered as he passed Mac (Lily, really) his pipe. She took it, confused but silent. Robert put his finger to her lips.

"What's going on?" Charlie asked.

Davy put his chin on Charlie's shoulder. "I think they're kissing again," he said.

"Let's get out of here." Charlie didn't feel well.

Davy looked back over the roof. It was a lot of area to cover without being seen. "How?" he asked, and rather cheerfully, too.

"Good question," boomed a voice from above.

"Robert, Robert what is it?" Mac called from the distance.

"You'd better come over here. I think I've discovered two Peeping Toms," said Dr. Robert Daniels.

"We're no Peeping Toms." Davy was indignant.

Mac picked her way across the moonlit roof and stood above the boys.

"Charlie, Davy, what on earth are you doing here?"

"We're not kissing, that's for sure," said Davy.

"That's enough from you, young man," snapped Dr. Daniels.

"Charlie, you have your operation tomorrow. If Nurse Butters finds out . . ." she let the thought trail. No need to say the rest. "Robert, we have to sneak them back into their beds."

"I was thinking of chucking them off the roof."

"Robert, that's not funny."

"Oh, was I being funny?"

"Robert, please, for Charlie's sake." Mac was beside herself.

"Yea, Robert, dear, give us a hand," sneered Davy. "After all, there's the little matter of you two kissing."

"Why, you little blackmailer."

"First you call me a Peeping Tom, even though we were here first, and now you call me a blackmailer." Dr. Daniels and Davy glared at each other.

"Stop it, both of you," said Mac. "It's Charlie's operation that's important here. Charlie honestly, I would have thought that you had more sense. As for you, Davy, don't be saucy. Charlie, stand up. Robert, you'll have to carry Davy. Let's go. Now."

Charlie stood up and looked away.

Mac and the little troupe tiptoed across the roof and down the same set of stairs she and Robert had used. The four popped out a door and landed one floor up from their ward. Mac walked away, quickly and purposefully, leaving the three to trail behind. At the end of the first hall she stopped, peeked around the corner, and motioned Robert, Davy, and Charlie forward. The four plunged down another set of stairs and once again set off.

Charlie tagged behind. Moving one leg in front of the other was the challenge. It wasn't fear he was feeling. It was something new, anger maybe. He stared at the back of Robert Daniels. There was something else — envy, maybe even hatred. What did his mother say about hating? It was hardest on those who carried it. But, for reasons he couldn't explain, he hated Dr. Robert Daniels.

Dr. Daniels shifted Davy in his arms.

"You know," said Davy to Dr. Daniels, "for a puny-looking egghead, you're rather strong."

"And you are a brat," muttered Robert.

Mac stopped short at the end of a hallway. The four clustered like bees. The ward was around the corner.

"All right, Nurse Butters is off duty. I think Rosabelle is on," whispered Mac. "If she is, we're in luck. I'll go down and tell her to take a break. When she passes by, you three come into the ward. Got it?" She gave them all a hard look.

Even Davy nodded his head obediently.

Mac charged ahead again, shoulders back, bold as brass. To be caught meant immediate dismissal without references for her, and heaven knows what would happen to Robert.

A minute later Rosabelle Brant, junior nurse, walked past at a brisk clip without so much as a glance in any direction.

"Come on, that's our cue," said Dr. Daniels, and the three slipped silently into the ward. Not counting old Christopher Adams' snore, not a soul made a sound.

Charlie hopped into bed, casting off his clothes as quick as he could. Robert lay Davy down gently and pulled the cover up over him. "We'll see you in the morning, then."

Davy didn't as much as say thank you.

Mac put Charlie's pillows right and collected his clothes.

"Sleep now, you hear. They'll be coming for you in just a few hours." Mac brushed Charlie's hair with her hand and whispered, "You're a funny one, Charlie Wilcox."

Charlie fixed his eyes on the far wall. "Charlie, what's the matter? No harm was done. Everything is all right," Mac kissed Charlie on the forehead. She smelled of lavender.

"As for you, Davy," Mac turned and stared down at the boy. "It was you that came up with this plan, wasn't it?" Davy said nothing. "What was it, Davy, did you just need to get out? Next time tell me, maybe I can help." Mac collected Davy's cast-off clothes too, bent down, and planted a kiss on Davy's forehead. Davy's mouth fell open in surprise. "Good night, Davy," said Mac.

"Night ol' chaps," said Dr. Daniels, and he and Mac melted away in the dark.

"Charlie, you asleep?"

"Yes."

"Charlie, maybe I was wrong about those two."

"Shut up."

Chapter 7

"Just breathe in, Charlie." The nurse held a golden-colored mask over his face. The ether went into his lungs and the room grew dim.

"No." Charlie pushed the mask away from his face. What was it? Operate on the wrong foot? Last night on earth? Charlie flung his arms around his face, like he was batting flies. "No, no."

"Now, Charlie, behave," said a voice from above.

Charlie caught a second whiff of ether. "No, away," sobbed Charlie. "Mac, she loves him. Dr. Daniels. They are in love. Kissing, on the roof. In love. Kissing."

"Just breathe in, Charlie. There's a good boy."

Charlie closed his eyes. He took a deep breath. The room grew dark.

HE WAS IN A SMALL rowing boat. The sea was still. No, not the sea but a large pond maybe. The water was inky black, the sky a deep blue with the morning sun on the horizon shooting streams of light up into the leftover dark. There was something floating in the water. Charlie's boat bumped into it. It was a body. He looked around. It wasn't one body, but hundreds of bodies — no, thousands of bodies. He reached into the water to touch one. He lifted it, lifted it high in the air. It was no body. It was a cat, a dead cat. The sea was filled with dead cats for as far as the eye could see.

"CHARLIE, CHARLIE, open your eyes. It's Mother. Charlie, open your eyes darling."

"THERE YOU GO. Come on, lift your head." Charlie followed Nurse Rosabelle's bossy voice up, up, and out of a sound sleep. His head ached and his mouth felt like a bale of hay had been parked in it.

"Mother?"

"Your mother had to leave, Charlie. Rules. But she's a stubborn one, your mother. Had a right catfight with Nurse Butters. Sat up in that hard chair all night, she did." Rosabelle motioned with her head to a mean-looking, hard-backed chair. She took his pulse and nodded in satisfaction.

"Mother?" The world was a blur.

"Don't you worry, you'll be fine. Got a headache, I don't wonder. Take this."

A gooey syrup slipped down his throat. Charlie choked,

swallowed some, and spat the rest up.

"Have a sip of water," said the nurse.

He felt a straw go into his mouth and a cool stream of water trickle down his throat.

"Back to sleep now."

"My foot?"

"The operation was a success, Charlie. Go back to sleep."

"Where is Mac?" Charlie fought to keep his eyes open.

"Don't you worry about that. Sleep now."

"SO, ARE YOU GOING to sleep the rest of your life or what? Wake up," snapped Davy.

"I'm awake." Charlie blinked and gazed around the room. "What are you doing?"

Pencils, and a large pad, were scattered over Davy's bed.

"None of your business. Look at this." Davy flung over a small brown booklet. It landed on Charlie's belly.

The cover of the catalog read, "Boston Artificial Limb Com-pany." And under the title it said, "The one you will eventually wear."

"Look on page six." Davy was so excited he near rolled out of his bed.

Charlie fumbled his way to the page.

"Read it."

"Our leather adjustable socket limb," Charlie paused, "made from plaster of Paris impression. Suitable for amputation below the knee. Price $85.00 net."

"That's it! My new legs. While you were sleeping, for a mere day and a half, I was getting fitted for new legs. Paid for by the Newfoundland Ladies Benevolent Society. What does *benevolent* mean?" Davy let out a yelp. "Who cares? A bunch of old toads, dressed up like black beetles, want to give me legs." Davy howled. "Hey, you awake or what?"

"It's good. Really good." He was so sleepy. "Where is Mac?"

"You should know. You were the one with the big mouth. Talked your head off, you did too. Just before they put you under. Blabbermouth Rosabelle told that other nurse, the one with the beak, all about it. I heard every word. Seems you told everything — how they were in love, kissing on the roof. Anyway, what do you think of my new legs?"

The book fell out of Charlie's hands and slid onto the floor.

"GOOD." Charlie put down his knife and fork.

"Well, boy, can't say as I've ever seen anyone eat hospital food so fast." Ol' Tom bellowed down the row of beds.

Charlie gave him a weak smile.

Three days had gone by since the operation. Today he'd walk on his new foot. Walk. Flat.

Dr. McKnight and his small fleet of young doctors were working their way down the row of beds.

"Davy, has anyone even said anything about Mac?" Charlie whispered.

"Nope." Davy busied himself with his pen and paper.

"Up you get, boy." Dr. McKnight sidled up to Charlie's bed.

With a great heave, Charlie sat up in bed and gingerly lowered his bare feet onto the floor. A shot of pain went up one foot.

"Oh," and Charlie pulled his poor foot back up. The operation didn't work.

"Come on, try again."

He lowered his feet once again, gently. The pain wasn't as awful this time.

Charlie stood on two flat feet. He couldn't move his ankle much, not at all really. But the foot was flat.

The ward let up a cheer.

"That's all for today," said Dr. McKnight. "Back into bed now. Nurse will be by to give your foot a little workout." And with that the troop of doctors moved back down the row and, with white coats flapping, barged out of the ward doors, like they were walking out of a saloon.

"Mac!" Charlie let out a yelp. There she was, all this time, standing off to one side. She must have come in behind the gaggle of doctors. At least it looked like Mac, from the neck up. But she was dressed peculiarly. She wore a veil on her head, a long gray robe with a red collar, and under it, a black skirt that near dusted the ground. And around her arm was a Red Cross armband. Behind her stood a man in an officer's uniform.

"Charlie, we've come to say good-bye," said Mac.

Charlie's mouth gaped open.

"We've joined up, Charlie, both of us. I'm with the Red Cross and Robert has joined the Medical Corps. There's a war on you know, in Europe." Tears rimmed Mac's eyes.

"Stay out of trouble, ol' boy." Dr. Daniels came around and tousled Charlie's hair.

"War? Why?" Charlie finally got two words out.

"Charlie," Mac whispered into his ear, "I'll think of you a lot. You take care. Do good things."

"But you don't have to go. It's my fault. I told."

"Whatever are you talking about?" Mac kissed him on his cheek.

"Take cover," whispered Davy as he cocked his head toward the top of the ward. "The enemy is approaching."

Sure enough, Nurse Butters was storming down the ward. Fury was in that woman's eyes.

"I believe you two," spoken directly to Mac and Dr. Daniels, "are no longer on staff at this hospital. And, as I'm sure you know, this is not Sunday. No visitors!"

Mac kissed Davy, quick like. And into Davy's ear she whispered, "Try to behave."

"Nurse Butters." Dr. Daniels met Nurse Butters' steely eyes with his own.

"Yes, Dr. Daniels?" Nurse Butters pursed her lips forward.

Suddenly, not giving Nurse Butters the time to duck, Dr. Daniels wrapped his arms around her and gave her a big, loud kiss on the lips. A cheer went up.

"How dare . . . how . . ." Nurse Butters, her face as pink as a fresh salmon, quivered with indignation. She pivoted on her heels and stomped off amongst cheers mingled with near hysterical laughter and applause.

"Good-bye there, mates." Dr. Daniels gave both boys a mock salute. "We'll be back soon enough. You'll see."

It was Ol' Tom who began it. Struggling to his feet, he started singing "The Ode to Newfoundland." One after the other, men climbed out of their beds and stood, as best they could, at attention. They sang as strong as men could sing with the last words of Cavendish Boyle's glorious song ringing out, "As loved our fathers, so we love. Where once they stood, we stand." And for a moment they were not sick, they were not left behind, they were united Newfoundlanders.

Tears streamed down Mac's face. Truth be told, there wasn't a dry eye in the house. Dr. Daniels put his arm around Mac, and the two listened to the song that they had heard, and loved, all their lives. And then Mac and her doctor were gone.

Charlie turned his face to the wall.

"YOUR PARENTS ARE WAITING downstairs, young man." Nurse Rosabelle handed Charlie his bag, the one Missus Eliza had given him on loan.

"Thank you." Charlie took it in one hand. Where was Davy?

Charlie walked past the row of beds. His foot worked all right. It wasn't perfect, not liked he'd hoped. There was a limp, but the hip-hop was gone. Charlie said his good-byes. He felt guilty, somehow, for leaving them all behind.

"Seen Davy?" he asked at the nurse's desk.

"I'm right behind you."

There stood Davy. On two legs.

"Look how tall I am." He grinned. Two crutches propped Davy up on either side, and an orderly stood ready with a wheelchair right behind him.

"They hurt like hell itself, but look." Davy slowly slid one foot forward. The orderly moved closer ready to catch him. "Get away," Davy snarled at the orderly. The second foot followed. Davy had taken his first step. "Whoooa!"

"Got you." Charlie held out his arms, wrapped them

around Davy, and helped him to sit in the waiting wheel-chair.

"You OK?"

Davy nodded.

"You aren't dying, are you?" Charlie looked Davy right in the eye.

"Of course I am. Ever heard of anyone getting out of this life alive? I'm just not planning on dying anytime soon. Let go of me." Davy shook Charlie off like a dog shakes water.

"You're off then?" Davy asked.

"I am."

"Yea well, have a good life."

"You too." Charlie stood, just stood, not knowing what to do. He picked up his valise and made for the door.

"Hey, Charlie," Davy wheeled up beside him. "Wait a minute. You once asked me how I lost me legs, but you never asked me why. It was a dare, Charlie. Me pal — he dared me to beat the streetcar and I fell. He never came to visit me, you know. Not once."

"Davy, I . . ." Charlie stammered.

"There's nothing to say. Here, I got something for you." Leaning back, careful like, Davy reached into the pocket of his robe and took out a rolled-up drawing. He handed it to Charlie. "I thought you might like it."

Gently, Charlie unrolled the scroll. It was a drawing of Mac! And not any old drawing either. A beautiful pencil drawing, and it looked just like her.

"Davy, you're an artist." Charlie was astonished.

"Naw, well, maybe." Davy grinned. "I made one of you, too, but I decided to keep that one. You take care now."

"Thank you. I will, Davy. And Davy," Charlie smiled, "guess wishes do come true, hu?" Charlie pointed to Davy's legs.

"Up your nose, bayboy."

Charlie laughed, folded the picture, slid it in his pocket, and walked out into the light of day.

"CHARLIE, MY SON," Skipper Sam stood on the grass, his arms stretched out in front of him.

Charlie ran, on two flat feet. Charlie ran as fast as he'd ever run in his whole life. Like his legs were spinning wheels. There was a limp, sure, but not much, not so as you could really tell.

"Father." Charlie fell into his father's arms and was crushed up against his rough woolen coat.

Sam's arms seem to surround Charlie twice over, like his dad couldn't hold him tight enough. "Thank you, God," said his father to the sky. "Thank you." Sam took a breath and stood back to get a look at his young son. "Well, now. Well, now. Come, your mother is just down the path."

Charlie walked beside his father. The sun was up and the day crystal clear. There was nothing stopping Charlie from following in his father's, and his grandfather's, footsteps. Not now, not with his foot right, almost right. He'd go to the ice now, sure as anything.

"Father, Mother was there, wasn't she? After the operation?" Charlie asked.

"She was indeed."

"It was hard on her, wasn't it? I mean, me being in the hospital."

"It was, my son, it was very hard."

"Why?"

"There's no harm in telling you now. When your mother was a girl, and her with her own mother not long dead, she came to this hospital, just built it was, with her baby sister. Her sister died here. But it was long ago now, Charlie. And now her son was fixed in this same place, so maybe she can put it behind her. Come on, let's not keep her waiting."

"Father, wait, I have to tell you something, about your spy glass."

Skipper Sam stopped short. "It's a beautiful thing. I was just cleaning it this morning. What put you in mind of it?"

Chapter 8

"You're not to think on it, Charlie. Not another word on the subject." Lucy's words came out of her mouth in frozen puffs. She plucked a crisp sheet from the line, gave it three smart folds, and dropped it in the wicker hamper.

"There's no reason why I can't go. My foot . . ."

"It has nothing to do with your foot. It never did. 'Go to the ice. Go to the ice.' I'm sick to death of hearing about it. Do you really know what that means?" Lucy pulled the next sheet off the line and pitched the pegs into a small basket. "My father was a sealer, and all my brothers. And before he became a captain, your own father sealed just like his brothers, and your grandfather, too. And I can tell you this, it's a hard life." Lucy ignored the cold March wind that whipped her face. She flung another folded sheet into the hamper.

"You'd be on the ice by 5:00 in the morning, six days a week, for weeks at a time. For twelve to sixteen hours, sometimes more, you'd be running from ice pan to ice pan, trying not to fall into water that will freeze the very blood in your veins. And if you do take a fall and two ice pans collide, you'll be cut in half. You'd be so shinnicked with the cold that the muscles in your body would move by their very selves! Can you fathom that, Charlie? Can you think on what it is to freeze where you stand? With fingers and toes so burnt they come off with your gloves and stockings! And then the hunt, it's not a pretty thing. A dog hood could cut you down soon as look at you. As for a white-coat, there's no sport in it."

It was all Lucy could do not to shake him. As the last sheet on the line flapped and cracked like a schooner sail being hoisted in the wind, Lucy took a deep breath. She knew this story so well.

"When you got back on the ship, you'd be gathering water to drink, standing watch, icing the pelts, and hauling coal to feed the ship's furnace. Think on it — shifting hundreds of tons of coal, by hand, in baskets. You'd be sleeping on wooden bunks, with only a homemade mattress filled with wood chips for comfort. And when you can get some sleep, chances are carcasses will drop through the hold, falling right on top of you. You'll wake up covered in blood and fat.

"You'd eat what you can cook, boiled salt cod maybe. And for breakfast you'd have a stew not fit for animals, let alone working men." Lucy put her hands on Charlie's shoulders and looked hard into her son's blue eyes. "Listen to me. I want you to have a chance at a better life, to go to the university."

"But, Mother," said Charlie, "It's been a good life for my father, and it's my life."

"Enough. You may be listening but you're not hearing." Lucy yanked the last sheet off the line and tumbled it into a ball. "I'm not saying that it's a bad life, I'm saying that there's more to living than hauling fish or going swilling. I'll hear no more talk on it." Lucy balanced the hamper on her hip and marched into the house.

"THAT'S THAT THEN." Claire Guy popped up from behind the water barrel. "What do you want to go to the ice for anyway? Sealing isn't any fun."

"Leave me alone. You don't understand." Charlie took to walking. Any direction would do so long as it led away from Claire.

"I do too understand," said Claire, as she trotted behind him. "You just want to be like all the rest. Go to the ice. But think on it, Charlie. If you go to the university you could get a real job, and we could move to the city."

Charlie stopped dead. "We?"

"Well," Claire measured her words, "just about everyone thinks we'll get married one day and . . ."

"Married?" Charlie was stunned. "I'm never getting married."

"Yes you will."

"If I do, I'm not going to marry you."

Claire marched up to Charlie and stood, bold as brass, not a breath from his face. "Says who? How do you know if you love me or not? You've never even kissed me."

"Kissed you?" Charlie's mouth went bone dry.

"Yea. Why don't you try it?" Claire caught hold of Charlie's hand and pulled him behind the water barrel where no one could see. She closed her eyes and puckered her mouth. She was no beauty, that was sure. "What are you waiting for?" Claire opened her eyes and glared at him. Boys were stupid and Charlie Wilcox was stupider than most. "Just make your mouth like this." Claire pursed her lips so far forward she looked like a mackerel. "Press your lips on mine. And go like this." Claire made a big, loud pop. "It's easy."

"That's not how it's done." Charlie said softly. He thought back to Mac, and her doctor, kissing on the roof of the hospital. It may have been dark, but he saw enough. He saw how the doctor put his arms around Mac's waist, how he pulled her into him, and how she turned her head just so. There was a gentleness there, and a need that he didn't yet understand. And they didn't make any disgusting popping sound like the top coming off a pot of jam.

"This is how you're supposed to do it." Charlie put his arms around Claire. "Put your arms around my neck." Claire's eyes turned into saucers — and her eyes were round to start with. He moved his head forward. They bumped noses.

"You have to turn your head to one side, like this," Charlie put his hands on either side of Claire's head and shifted it slightly to the left. "Now don't move, and don't make your mouth all funny. OK, ready?"

Charlie kissed her. Her mouth felt soft.

Claire's arms went around Charlie, her hands drifted up and down his back, hands that didn't seem to belong to her anymore. He kissed her once, a long kiss, and then again, and again, short quick kisses.

All in all, Charlie found it a much nicer experience than he had expected.

"How do you know how to do that?" Shaken, Claire drew back her head. "Who have you been kissing?"

"No one . . . I . . ."

"You're a liar, Charlie Wilcox. You've been kissing someone else. I can tell. Who was it? No, don't tell me. Don't ever speak to me again." And there she went, back straight, arms flying back and forth, marching she was, out of the yard and into the street.

Charlie looked around. No one saw. He plopped down on the back step. That didn't go very well.

"Charlie, Charlie." Emma swung the back door open so wide it near knocked Charlie senseless.

"Ouch! I'm here."

"Well, what are you sitting there for? You'll get piles on that cold step." It wasn't like Emma was wanting an answer or nothing 'cause words just kept flying out her mouth.

"Your mother wants you to fetch your father home from the Jubilee Club. Your great-aunt Maude is coming all the way from St. John's. No warning. Honestly. Well, what are you waiting for? Go!"

Aunt Maude. Aunt Maude had more money than God, and she was always butting in. But with two sons grown, one gone to Canada, the other to America, and herself a widow, maybe she had nothing better to do. Whatever she was here for, it was for nothing good.

Charlie yanked his cap out from his back pocket and pulled it down low over his forehead. The club wasn't far, just around the corner. Besides, he liked to walk, to stride, to take giant steps and small ones, too. Just the feeling of putting one foot in front of the other made him feel light and free. The limp was there, slight, but no bother, none a'tall.

THE JUBILEE CLUB was in a little white house, but it was a club all right, with billiards and card tables. Of course, only the leading men of the town were members. No woman ever darkened its door, and since spirits were served, lads like Charlie had only glimpsed the inside. Young Bill Wright, who was pushing sixty, ran it just fine after his father passed over.

"Here for your father?" Young Bill came out the back door carrying two buckets of slop for the pigs.

Charlie nodded.

"Go on in then and give a shout."

Charlie ducked into the kitchen and crept down the passage. Wasn't often he got this far without being hauled back.

"It'll be over anytime now, anytime."

"Ach, we may have been in this war from the beginning, but our boys haven't yet had a fair crack at the Huns. They'll get it then. Show the Brits up, too, I'll wager. No one is as tough as a Newfoundlander."

"Sam, what about young Charlie, too young to join up?"

"I'd say so. The boy is just fourteen. Wouldn't matter if he was twenty-five. His mother won't let him go to the ice," boomed back Skipper Sam. "I expect she'd have something to say on him going to war."

"A Wilcox not go to the ice? Sam, every Wilcox ever born on this land has gone to sea. Shame to stop a tradition now." Charlie recognized Mister Lambe's voice right off.

"His mother has other plans for him," said Skipper Sam. "He's to go to St. John's and finish school, then to the university. Besides," Sam took a draw from his pipe, "he's not a strong boy. He's not made for the ice."

Charlie stood as still as a boy ever stood.

Not made for the ice? Not made for the ice? Like his ears could hear the words but his brain couldn't take them in. It was as good as a belly blow, as good as any whack Clint had ever given him. Charlie wrapped his arms around his stomach. Not made for the ice? He spun around and headed for the light at the end of the hall.

"He can do better," said Skipper Sam to all those who could hear. "He's a smart one and he's got guts. And I'll tell you this," Sam leaned over the table and grinned, "I know that boy. He'll do all of Brigus proud."

But Charlie was long gone. Out to the yard. Past Young Bill and his pails and his pigs. He ran all the way home, through the door, up the stairs, into his room, and fell into his bed. He folded the pillow around his head.

Every Wilcox that had ever lived in Newfoundland had gone to the ice. If he didn't go to the ice then he wasn't a Wilcox. And if he wasn't a Wilcox, who was he? The word *coward* kept coming back to him, like an echo. A weak coward not fit for the ice. And everyone would know.

Charlie took a breath. He looked around his room. On the dresser stood a framed picture of Robert Bartlett, Bob they called him, captain like his father. Explorer. Took Perry to the Pole. Whole world knew about Captain Bob. He'd sail with him, sure as anything, Charlie Wilcox would sail with Bob Bartlett. The tears soaked his pillow. The room grew dim and after a while Charlie fell asleep.

"CHARLIE, CHARLIE, you up there?"

Charlie flopped over onto his back and gazed at the ceiling of his room. He was tired, every bone and then some, felt like lead. The room was dark.

"Charlie?" Emma stood at the door huffing from the climb. "What's a'matter with you? You sick?" As usual Emma didn't wait for an answer. "Everyone is at the table. Hurry up."

Emma turned and stomped down the stairs. Maybe she wouldn't marry Murphy Milford. Anyway, he said he was going to join up and have some fun with the Huns. Well, he could go off and have his fun. If it wasn't to be Murphy, she'd marry someone else, anyone, as long as she got a house of her own. And when she did, by God Hisself, she'd run her house proper like. No sniveling kids for her.

Charlie pulled himself up, poured water into the basin, and splashed it on his face. The cold water stunned him for a second. He looked into the spotty, old mirror above the washstand. Not fit for the ice.

"THERE YOU ARE!" Lucy stood at the bottom of the stairs. She was dressed in her best, a dark brown sash over a cream-colored dress with a lacy front. Sam had brought it back for her from New York City. "We looked all over for you. Didn't Emma send you to fetch your father?" Lucy licked her fingers and patted down Charlie's hair. Charlie winced. He hated when she did that. "Never mind, he's here now. Aunt Maude is here, too. Oh, and Claire came by so I asked her to stay for dinner."

Well, his mother was being awfully jolly. Glad somebody was happy.

"What's wrong?" Lucy peered into Charlie's eyes.

"Nothing." Charlie brushed past his mother and went into the dining room.

The incandescent light made the whole room brighter than it should have been. Stretched out, and running the length of the room, was a long, narrow table. It could sit two dozen or more when it had to. It was all dressed up with the best Irish linen, crystal glasses, and some flowery china that his father had brought back from England. It was all the same to Charlie but visitors gushed over it.

Two lamps stood on the sideboard, each fringed with pale pink beads that danced and dangled in the light. Charlie's grandfather, Moses, glared down from an oval, gilded frame on the wall just above the lamps. It was Moses' grandfather who was the first Wilcox to reach the shores of Newfoundland. You wouldn't want to do much wrong with the eyes of Moses watching you. At the head of the table stood his father, handsome, brave, strong, respected.

Charlie slumped down in the only empty chair in the room — the one beside Claire. For reasons Charlie could not fathom, Claire was strangely quiet. Father carried on, carving a turkey the size of a small cow. As for Charlie's two sisters, they paid him no mind, seldom did.

"So, Charles," Aunt Maude focused her beady eyes on Charlie. "I hear your foot is fixed. Now you're a regular boy." Aunt Maude was stout, even her chins were stout, all three of them. Charlie was counting.

"Hello, Aunt Maude," Charlie mumbled.

"Give your Aunt Maude a kiss, Charlie," Lucy smiled from the foot of the table, then she shot Charlie a hard look.

Charlie squeezed between the backs of the chairs and the sideboard. He leaned forward, kissed Aunt Maude's soft face, and came away with powder on his lips. Aunt Maude smelled sour, like turned, sugared cream. Very odd.

Charlie slumped back in his chair and looked neither left nor right. For the first time in his life, Charlie could not look his father in the eye.

"Well, not an auspicious start I must say," declared Aunt Maude.

Charlie had no idea what *auspicious* meant, and he didn't care.

"Charlie, Aunt Maude has come to make you a very generous offer," his father spoke gently. "She would like you to go back with her and finish up high school in St. John's."

"The Methodist College," Lucy jumped in. "Where Captain Bob Bartlett went."

"He didn't stay. Captain Bob quit," said Charlie, more sarcastically than he meant to.

Aunt Maude tisk-tisked and Sam cleared his throat before continuing.

"After you graduate from the Methodist College you can go on to the university. Mount Allison maybe."

No, never. I'm never going to go live with her. I'm not going to that college and I'm not going to the university. I'm not and you can't make me. I'm going to the ice. But Charlie didn't say that, not a'tall.

"Charlie, it's a great opportunity," said Lucy. Her voice was strained. The look on her face, with pleading eyes and jaw pulled tight, made her look pained, like someone was stepping on her foot.

Charlie thought on it. A plan — just the beginnings sure, but a plan nevertheless — was forming in his head. Claire kicked him.

"When do I have to go?" piped up Charlie, too brightly.

A cheer went up.

"Oh, Charlie." Lucy flew around the table and hugged her son. Relief, honest relief, spread around the room. He would be safe from the ice.

"A good decision, my son," laughed Sam with a smile so broad his eyes near vanished. "Now, will that be white meat or dark, Aunt Maude?"

"You never had much of a memory, Samuel. I trust next time you'll remember that I only eat white meat."

"White it is." Sam smiled and sliced off a side of turkey. "And, Charlie, since this is a special occasion, why don't I give you an extra helping of figgy duff?" Sam plopped the flour, raisins, and molasses mixture on the plate, and doused it liberally with the brown sugar sauce. The plate was passed to Claire, who plunked it in front of him.

"That was too easy," Claire hissed in Charlie's ear. "What are you thinking? I can hear you thinking."

"Can not."

"Oh, yes I can. Charlie Wilcox, you are up to something."

"Will you two stop whispering," Lucy laughed. She was in a very gay mood now. "Eat up."

Aunt Maude, Lucy, and Skipper Sam went on and on about details. There were things to be worked out, school registration, uniforms, books. Charlie's sisters prattled on about the upcoming church bazaar. Emma came in and cleared away the supper dishes, none too quietly either.

"Charlie, you're very quiet," said Lucy. "Why don't you take Claire into the parlor? We'll have coffee in there."

IN THE SITTING ROOM, and behind glass, sat the polished and gleaming spy glass. Charlie could hardly take his eyes off of it. It was there the day Charlie got back from the hospital. And on that very day he had asked Jim Norton how it got back there.

"Don't know," Jim had said. "I was guarding the glass, like you said, when up the path comes Clint. So I charged down to meet him — didn't want him seeing the glass like. Got beat up real good, and then ran down to get help. And there you were, getting on a train! What was I to do? My mother got hold of me and by the time I got back up Grave Hill, the glass was gone. Just gone! The next thing I knew, it was back in your parlor!"

From that day to this, how the spy glass found its way home was a mystery.

"What are you looking at?" Claire knew full well since Charlie's eyes were glued to the spy glass.

"Nothing. I'm just remembering something," said Charlie.

Claire smiled.

And then Charlie knew.

"It was you!"

"Me what?"

"You got the glass down. You went up Grave Hill and got it. You brought it here!"

"It took you long enough."

Charlie looked at Claire, looked real hard.

"Now, tell me what you are planning," demanded Claire.

"I'm not planning anything."

"You are a liar, Charlie Wilcox, and a lie has more lives than a cat. You want to go to the ice, I know you do. You're not giving in that easy." Claire put her hands on her hips and rooted her feet to the floor.

"I'm going to St. John's. That's that," said Charlie, although he didn't dare look her straight in the face.

"I don't believe you," whispered Claire, "and you haven't even said thank you."

"You two certainly have your heads together," laughed Lucy as she led the way into the sitting room. "Take the soft seat, Aunt Maude. The girls will be in with the coffee."

"What are you looking at, Charlie?" Skipper Sam followed the ladies into the room. "Ah, the spy glass. You remember this old glass, Aunt Maude? Came over with your grandfather, my great-grandfather." Sam reached past Charlie and opened the glass cabinet. "Been passed from father to son ever since. And maybe it's time . . ." Skipper

Sam paused and smiled at Charlie, "that I pass it on to Charlie."

Silence. Except for the distant murmur of his sisters giggling in the kitchen, no one said a word.

"But Sam . . . do you think . . . ?" Lucy's voice trailed off.

"Tradition has it that you're to get it when I die, Charlie. Now I ask you . . ." Sam beamed at his wife, "what fun do I have in that?"

"Well, if you want my opinion," sniffed Aunt Maude, "you're being impulsive as usual, Samuel Wilcox. He's just a boy. He'll lose it."

"What do you say, my son? Do you want the glass?" Sam held the spy glass out to Charlie.

Charlie could feel a gallon of tears just waiting to fall out. He blinked and reached for the glass. His, it belonged to him. And yet, why would his father give it to him if he was not fit to go to sea?

"I'll never lose it. I promise," Charlie whispered.

"What was that? Speak up, boy!" Aunt Maude barked.

"I said," he repeated loudly, "I'll never lose it."

"I know you won't, Charlie. It could be in no better hands." All the parts of Skipper's face smiled, his mouth, his eyes, his cheeks. "And when you learn to see through that glass, mind I said *see* and not *look* — when you can see with your heart, your soul, and your eyes, when you focus on what's ahead with every part of you — then you will be a sailor."

"Thank you." Charlie ran his hand over its surface.

"Might want to thank me, too," Claire muttered, but only so Charlie could hear.

"I think this calls for something a little stronger than coffee. How about a glass of blueberry wine, Aunt Maude? Lucy makes the best in Brigus." There was no happier man in Brigus than Sam Wilcox that night.

"I don't normally partake, as you know, Sam, but why not toast your foolishness?" Aunt Maude adjusted the buttons on the blouse that covered her big bosom.

"Three glasses then." Skipper Sam pulled a decanter from the sideboard. He looked at Charlie and Claire. "Well, maybe we'll make it five glasses, just this once."

Sam took a decanter from the sideboard, poured out the sweet, near black, blueberry wine, and handed the glasses around.

With a flourish Sam held his glass high. "To my son, the first university graduate in the family."

"I hear it again," whispered Claire.

"What?"

"You're thinking. And it's not good."

Chapter 9

$\mathcal{W}$ith less fanfare than might be expected, Charlie was packed off to St. John's.

"You behave." Lucy stood at the front door and fidgeted with Charlie's collar. "And write." Charlie knew the look on his mother's face really well. It was the same stoic face she reserved for Skipper Sam when he was heading off to sea. No smile, no frown, not an emotion could be seen, only the muscles around her jawline pulled tight.

Sam shook Charlie's hand once, then shook his hand all over again. "It's for the best." If he had said that once, he had said it a hundred times over the past two weeks. Sam took charge of Charlie's small steamer trunk. It was the blue one with the brass trim and leather grips — best in the house. Emma held Charlie's haversack out to him with two pinched fingers, like it was stinky.

"What's in here?" she asked, then she shook it furiously.

"Get off." Charlie hissed as he grabbed the bag. Jeeze, she was always poking her pug nose into his things.

The journey to St. John's held no surprises. Charlie sat on the red velvet seat in the first-class coach and looked out at the passing land. His land, his country. But it was a dull day, the sun hardly bothering to make an appearance. And Charlie felt as listless, almost sad, as the day looked.

On the train, off the train, and here he was, standing on the platform waiting for Aunt Maude.

"Yooo-who, Charlie, over here!"

Aunt Maude came flouncing down the train platform. Her purple skirt was a circle of frills, while the top part of her round body was laced up like a sausage.

"I'm glad to see that you are on time. I don't hold with tardiness," said Aunt Maude without so much as a smile.

"No ma'am." As if Charlie had any control whatsoever over the train's arrival.

"Have you got everything?" Aunt Maude looked over his haversack and small trunk. There was little to complain about, pity.

"Yes, ma'am."

"Then we're off."

A motorized taxi waited at the curb just outside the train station. Whoa! If Jim Norton could see him now! The driver stood beside the opened door. Charlie made a dive for the back seat.

"Hold on there, boy, you're not in the bay now. Ladies first. Stand back." It proved to be a good idea since Aunt

Maude's backside required a great deal of room. The two settled in and, after a backfire, they were off in a shower of smoke.

They drove past the harbor. Dozens of ships, most docked, some anchored out in the bay, rocked impatiently on the water. Charlie stuck his head out the window to get a better view. The sight of them near took his breath away.

"Look there," Charlie pointed to men on the dock — hundreds of them all lined up clutching boxes and papers.

"Get your head in this instant, young man, and do not point. What has your mother been doing with her time? Have you not seen men waiting on their tickets before? It's the sealing they're in for, I expect."

"No, I was looking at the soldiers." To one side of the docks soldiers lulled about, their jackets opened, puttees pulled up smartly or bunched around ankles.

"A fine bunch they are, too," said Aunt Maude. "I expect they'll see little action. Just a bunch of lads off for adventure. Of course, my sons, your second cousins, will have none of this nonsense, and good thing, too." Aunt Maude's voice trailed off for a second. "But those soldiers do cost, I'll tell you. We'll bankrupt the country just so those boys can have some fun. Can't think how that bill will be paid. Still, God and country, and there can be no finer man on earth than the King. And," said Aunt Maude with her finger pointed right at Charlie's nose, "we do have to teach those Huns a lesson."

"Are they very bad?"

"Who?"

"The Huns. Are they terrible?"

"Oh goodness knows. I knew a German once. Nice

enough fellow. As the war keeps going on, I expect we'll
come to believe that all Germans are monsters. It's easy to
kill a monster now, isn't it? If we thought they were just
like us, with wives and children and such — well, how
would we shoot them? But it's not for the likes of you and
me to bother about. Here we are." The motorized taxi came
to a begrudging halt and the two passengers shot forward,
then back, before they themselves came to a stop.

"Annie! Cook! Open this door at once." Aunt Maude
was hollering before she even set foot out of the taxi.
"Come along, Charlie. You can't sit in there all day." The
front door swung open and Aunt Maude stomped up
the steps. "I must retire for a few repairs," said Aunt
Maude. "Annie will take care of you. Annie," she bellowed.
"Annie!"

"Yes, ma'am," a small lady, a girl, really, with a round
pink face and curly red hair escaping from her maid's cap,
popped out from behind the opened door.

"Oh, you're always sneaking up on me," Aunt Maude
sputtered. Annie must have heard that before because her
only reaction was the teeniest, weeniest little smile. "This
is my great-nephew, Charles Wilcox. See to his luggage."
And with that Aunt Maude disappeared into the grand
house to do, what? What would she repair?

"Come along," said Annie. She had a strong accent. Irish
maybe. Charlie helped the driver with his trunk and then
stood, hat in hand, at the entrance of the grand home.
"Welcome, Master Charles. Dinner is near ready," said
Annie. "Sure, don't you be worrying about your trunk just
now. Just you sit down in the drawing room for a bit and

have a wee rest after your long journey. When your auntie returns, dinner will be served."

"Thank you," said Charlie.

Annie opened two massive doors and Charlie found himself in a large pink room — well, not pink exactly nor red either, more like the color of a ripe plum. Instead of his mother's bright, cheery parlor that invited the sunlight in, the drapes in Aunt Maude's house almost blocked the sun out entirely. Velvet curtains, as deep and dark a red as you could ever imagine, hung down over the windows. They looked like something out of Mister Lambe's butcher shop. And high up, near the ceiling of the powerful high room, were great swags of material that threatened to take a tumble and suffocate anyone passing by.

It was packed with overstuffed chairs, hassocks, and sofas. Each one was smothered in fat flowers — floral chintz his mother would have said. Jeeze, Charlie thought, a person only had one behind, how come there were so many places to park it?

Bad enough that every wall was covered with pink, red, and gray velvet wall-coverings, but on top of that were dozens of gold-framed portraits. Miserable-looking men, not a happy or kind face amongst them. Just the look of them might scare a person witless.

Beside each chair was a spindly side table, and on top of the tables, cranberry glass lamps fringed with dancing prisms. In fact, every tabletop and book shelf was crammed with ruby-colored glasses.

Charlie sat down on the edge of a hassock and tried not to move. A breath sent the wrong way might topple the lot.

"Well, Charles, this is your new home." Aunt Maude stood, proud and priss, at the doorway. "I hope you are comfortable. Come, it's time to dine. You may escort me in." Aunt Maude slowly turned around, rather like a ship showing off her stern.

Charlie scurried up beside her and cocked his arm up, like he had seen his dad offer his arm to his mother. Aunt Maude reached for it. Off they sailed into the dining room, Aunt Maude under full steam.

Jeeze, but there was a fine feed on the sideboard. Eggs and sausages and fish and some sort of chicken, too. Charlie dove for his chair, tucked his napkin under his chin, and made ready to tear in.

"Humm," Aunt Maude cleared her throat while standing beside her chair.

Jeeze! Charlie clean forgot about pulling out Aunt Maude's chair. He raced around and yanked the chair out. Aunt Maude, with some fanfare, sat down. Thump.

"We have work to do on you," she sniffed as she gave her napkin a shake. "Annie," Aunt Maude bellowed. "Bring over that serving plate." And to Charlie she said, "She goes by the name of Annie. She's Irish."

Annie, standing not two feet away, gave Charlie a weak smile.

"They're not nearly as dirty as some say, you know — the Irish, I mean." Aunt Maude took aim and pierced a hard-boiled egg with the intent of doing it harm. The egg shot across Aunt Maude's plate. Aunt Maude gave chase with her fork.

"Annie, tell Cook that the eggs are overdone, again. Eat

up, Charles. Just you think of those starving children in Europe."

Aunt Maude believed in eating for those who could not. She plucked a fat kipper off the plate and landed it, with great skill, on her own plate. Charlie watched as she almost consumed the fish in one, maybe two bites. She did not refer to any repairs she had made, but even Charlie, who seldom noticed this sort of thing, could see that she had applied a new layer of powder to her face. Several layers, as a matter of fact. Most of it now lay creased in the folds under her chins.

"Annie, bring me my purse," ordered Aunt Maude between bites.

Annie placed a bead-crusted purse beside Aunt Maude's elbow.

"Charles, now that you are a young gentlemen, you'll need to carry a few coins in your pocket." Aunt Maude dumped the purse's contents onto the white linen table-cloth and separated out four Newfoundland shillings. She placed them top side up so George V's sour face looked back at them. "And this is from your parents." Aunt Maude plunged one hand into her bosom and fished out four crisp dollar bills. Charlie's breath went in and didn't come out. He reached for them. They were still warm.

"Thank . . ."

"No sense thanking me. Write your parents and thank them." That done, Maude pushed the remaining coppers back in her purse, snapped it shut, and dabbed her chins with a napkin. It was on to the next course — a whacking, great chicken with its cooked head still attached.

Chapter 10

"Master Charlie, darlin', are ya ready for yer bed?" asked Annie, as she turned down his bedclothes.

"I can help." Charlie ran round the other side of the bed, and together the two folded up the top bedcover. That done, Charlie, dressed in his flannelette, ankle-length night-robe, looked out his bedroom window while Annie fussed about. A trellis, thick with ivy, was beside his window. Charlie reached out and gave it a shake. It seemed sturdy enough.

"Are you thinkin' about yer family? Sure, don't I know a thing about that. It's been two years since I left Belfast, and there's not a day that goes by, not an hour . . ." Annie bit her lip and pulled back the blankets on young Master Charles' bed. "I got a letter from my mother not three weeks ago," she carried on. "Three of my brothers have joined up. The Ulster Regiment. My . . ." said Annie in a whisper, "what I wouldn't give to see them in uniform." A shiver went down her spine. "Ach, someone has walked over my grave, sure." Annie belted the pillows. "There you are now, Master Charles. Get you to your bed. I hear your tutor will be here first thing in the morning. That's a very fine thing, to have a tutor of your own. You'll have to work very hard to get ready for high school in the fall. Very good school I hear. Sleep well." And she was gone.

Charlie crept across the carpeted floor and opened his bedroom door a smidgen. He peered down the hall. All was quiet.

Now, thought Charlie.

He peeled off his night-robe and stood, fully dressed, in the middle of the room. Charlie plumped the pillows, laid them down the bed, and tossed a blanket over the lot. There was the slim chance that Aunt Maude would peek in to say good night. Next, Charlie dragged his haversack out from under the bed. He gave it a check. Mittens, long johns, his warmest oil-slick sweater, jacket, and the wool hat his mother gave him last Christmas. Then there were the boots. He tied the laces in a knot and flung them over his shoulder. Years back, his father had worn these same boots. They were sealer's boots studded with sharp sparables and chisels (hobnails and metal strips). You'd not be long standing on an ice pan wearing regular boots.

He had a pot, mug, knife, and fork. And food, too — two bags of hard tack, three apples, a bag of rolled oats, and raisins from home, and a couple of soft buns swiped from Aunt Maude's table. The only thing missing was his own iron-tipped gaff hook, but there was no way to sneak that past his mother and father, let alone Emma.

Charlie pushed his four dollars deep into his pocket and the four coins along with them. Carefully, he folded and slipped in the drawing Davy had done of Mac. One more thing. Charlie flung open the wardrobe and pulled down the spy glass. He wrapped it in his oil-slick sweater and jammed it into his haversack. He was ready — almost ready.

Charlie reached into his back pocket and pulled out a letter. It was addressed to his parents. It didn't say much, only that he was going to the ice and they were not to worry. Charlie leaned it up against a lamp.

In no time Charlie was out the window and down the trellis.

The streets of St. John's looked mean by the light of electric street lamps. Charlie paused and shivered, but he wasn't cold. This was it. He was doing it, actually doing it. All he had to do was keep doing it. One foot in front of the other. He looked back at Aunt Maude's house, then up to his opened bedroom window. Even if he wanted to, getting back in the house would be a lot harder than getting out. No, he had to do this.

Charlie followed the route that the taxi had taken that very morning. Down and down he went toward the harbor. Occasionally he'd come to a hump in the road, then it flattened out, only to dip back down again. Charlie reached Water Street. Barroom doors opened and for a second laughter and light spilled out onto the street. The doors closed and there was quiet again. Water lapped up against the docks, lazy water. In the moonlight, it looked like sheets of black, pitted metal.

There was nothing to do but wait. Charlie crawled behind a wooden barrel, crouched down low, and waited for the sun to come up, for his chance to stow away on an ice-bound ship.

"YA GET OUT of the line, boys, and ya be out." The sheer blast of the harbormaster's voice all but rattled Charlie's teeth. Jeeze, he must have dozed off.

Like a fox from its fox hole, Charlie poked his head up and looked around. The sun was up, well almost. The dock was filling up with hard-faced men, all with the intent of getting a berth, a ticket they called it, and going to the ice. Each had a gaff hook in one hand and a sealing box hoisted on his shoulder, or lying like an anchor at his feet. Everything a man needed to stay alive, body and soul, was in that box, packed by the wife, the mother. Even food. Salted beef, boiled eggs maybe, all wrapped up.

Lines formed behind makeshift tables. Papers were shown, one man got a berth, another rejected. Wooden-wall ships, old and worn, were anchored cheek-by-jowl, beside the pride of the Arctic — the SS Florizel and the SS Bellaventure, both steamers. It was a beautiful sight.

"What we got here? Bit small for a rat." Clint Miller looked down at Charlie and grinned ear-ta-ear.

Chapter 11

"Get away from me, Clint." Charlie jumped up smartly and puffed himself up as big as he could.

He needn't have bothered. Clint wasn't about to start anything. A ruckus on the docks would have them both turffed off, and Clint was meaning to get a berth this season.

"Calm down, Hoppy-boy." Clint lowered his voice. "Is it a berth that you want?"

"None of your bloody business and my foot works fine," hissed Charlie.

"Oh, that's right. I almost forgot. Now we'll just call you Flat-foot."

That was it. Charlie sent the barrel he was hiding behind into a spin and took a swing.

"Whooo. You stupid, little beggar. Want to get us both kicked off?" Clint looked over his shoulder.

Charlie studied Clint, looked past him at the line-ups, and, for the first time ever, both boys were in agreement.

"Look here. I know it's a berth that you want, but you've got no papers, right, boy?" Clint sneered. "I can tell ya how ta board her. And I'll tell ya where ta hide."

"Why?"

"How much ya got?"

"That depends."

"Look you . . ." Clint hissed, then collected himself. "Charlie-boy, for a price, I'll help you out. It's business. Now, how much do you got?"

Charlie reached into his pocket and fingered his precious four dollars. He reached down deeper and held out two Newfoundland shillings.

"What's this? This is all you have? Don't make me laugh." Clint tossed his head back and turned to walk away. Charlie held fast and counted Clint's steps. One, two — if he reached six, Charlie would yell out after him and give over a dollar. Three, four. Clint turned back.

"All right. I'll help you out of the goodness of my heart. Listen good." Clint grabbed the two shillings and jammed them into his own pocket. "You stay put. I'm just going to scout around." Clint sauntered away, hands in his pockets, a whistle on his lips, like he hadn't a care in the world. Charlie slipped back down behind the barrel.

"WAKE UP!" Clint gave the barrel a kick. He was back all right, with a gleam in his eye.

107

"I wasn't asleep." Charlie rubbed his eyes.

"See those crates down there on the dock?" Clint knelt down beside Charlie.

Charlie looked and nodded.

"Well, they're going to be loading them onto that ship down there any time now. This is how I see it. You get in a crate. Once the ship has sailed, you're on yer own, boy. When she's well on her way, out you come!"

That sounded simple enough — too simple.

"How will we get one of the crates opened?" Charlie asked.

Clint said not a word, just held up his gaff hook.

"It's done, me boy. I just popped it open like the lid on your mother's pickle jar. Pop." Clint made a sucking sound. "Get your stuff. Follow me and walk like you mean it. Like you belong here." Clint grinned. "And if you get caught, it's nothing to do with me. Got it?"

Charlie nodded, dumbly.

Clint grinned again. It might work. And if it didn't, who cared!

Clint walked the length of the dock; Charlie tagged behind him. A lone, young soldier stood guard near the crates.

"I'll distract the guard. You crawl into that crate. See the one that's part opened?" Clint motioned with his head. "Think you can do that, Flat-foot?"

Charlie nodded.

Clint stopped, took a pinch of tobacco out of a small leather bag, and rolled himself a cigarette. He walked up to the young guard and offered him one, friendly like, but not too friendly. As much as he strained, Charlie couldn't hear a word.

The guard seemed happy to talk. He'd been watching the crates for hours now. They were each big enough to hold a horse, and it wasn't likely the things were going to walk away on their own. The guard bent down for the light in Clint's cupped hand. Clint gave the nod in Charlie's direction.

With his heart going a mile a minute, Charlie crept behind the crates. Sure enough, one was open. The word "explosives" was written on the side. Charlie paid it no mind. It was common enough. All fishing ships heading for the ice carried explosives. If the ship got frozen into the ice, well, they'd blow up the ice to set the ship free.

Charlie threw his haversack into the crate and crawled in after it. There wasn't much room, but he fit all right, as long as he didn't move around too much. He put his hands around the wooden slats of the crate and pulled them toward him. The nails slipped back into the holes.

"Attention!"

Charlie froze.

"What's this, soldier?" A burly man, shaped like a barrel with the head of a walrus perched on top, barked at the young soldier. Clint melted away.

"Nothing, sir." That was all Charlie could hear of the young guard's retort.

"Charlie, you in there?" Clint hissed through the slats.

"Yea."

"Good lad. Stay put." Clint gave the nails on the crate a swift pound with a rock. "They are going to load these things any time now. Have a good trip." And Clint was gone. And Charlie was left. All that was to do now was doze, which he did.

IT WAS THE SHOUTING that woke him. One fisherman yelled something or other. An engine revved up. Not a ship's engine. Something else entirely. There was a sort of high-pitched squeal, then, a *caaa-chunk*! Mighty clamps took hold of either side of the crate and up he went.

"Whooo." Charlie closed his eyes. He felt sick. There he was, hovering in the air, swinging and swaying. More swinging. More swaying. "Whooo." No noise. No noise. Charlie stuffed a fist in his mouth. His stomach flipped and flipped again. Then *thunk*. The crate landed. Charlie peeked out through the slats. He must be on the deck.

"Careful there, boys, it's explosives you're playing with. Don't want them going off before we're ready." Charlie hadn't thought of that.

Then up again, into the air, and just as suddenly, he was plunged into darkness. Charlie was in the cargo hold of the ship, had to be. A second crate came crashing down on top of the one he was in. One by one, crates filled up the hold. There was no turning back now.

THE BUSTLE carried on for half a day, not that Charlie had much of a way to measure time. And then the doors up top were closed and the hold of the ship was plunged into total darkness. Now all he had to do was wait.

Sometime later the boilers were stoked and the pistons

began to grind. "I made it. I made it. I made it. I made it," whispered the pistons. Charlie's heart pumped right along with the beat. "Ya-hoooo." Charlie hollered, then laughed. There was no one to hear him now. And anyway, it wasn't like he'd get into too much trouble. Oh sure, he'd get a talking to from the captain but stowaways were considered good luck — and free labor.

Hours went by. Days for all Charlie knew. He mopped his forehead with his sleeve. The heat from the boilers left him near breathless. If he could just . . . Charlie reached up above him and pressed his back against the top of the crate. It didn't budge. He tried again and again. He peered through the slats. It was pitch black.

"I can do this." Talking out loud helped. "I can do this." With his back up against one side of the crate, Charlie pulled his legs into his chest and gave the side of the crate a mighty thump. The nails wiggled in the holes, but that wasn't the real trouble — it was the other crates pressing against the one he was in. Again, and again, he thumped at the sides. Nothing. "No worry," Charlie muttered. "No worry," as if to convince himself. It wouldn't take long now, to reach the ice, thought Charlie. Someone would come down, soon.

Charlie dozed more than slept. His legs ached. The heat was the worst. He took off his shirt and his socks. If he scrunched his body up against the wood, he could reach back into his pack. The buns and apples went fast. He scraped his teeth against the hard tack.

"Hello," he called out. And later, "Help."

The drone of the pistons drowned out even the loudest voice.

Chapter 12

It was a dream Charlie was in. There he was, standing on Bishop's Beach in Brigus. It wasn't a proper beach at all — not a grain of sand in sight. Only smooth, round rocks along the shoreline. He watched as the waves rolled in. Each one brought with it something from the sea. A boot. A bloated, dead fish with bloody eyes. A deck chair. And like it was made of wood, a steel anchor.

"Give us a cig there, Michael."

"You want to have a smoke atop forty thousand pounds of ammo?" Michael chuckled. "Just check the lashings."

Michael held the flashlight while Martin gave the ropes that secured the crates a good tug.

"All secure," said Martin.

"Let's go." Michael flashed the light on the hatch.

The door to the hold banged shut and the voices were gone.

"Hello," Charlie called out.

Silence. There were no voices. He had dreamed it. Charlie fell back into a dull, thick sleep.

"I TELL YA, I heard something." Martin opened the door to the hatch and shone the flashlight around the hold.

"You heard nothing. Come on, we'll be late." Michael stood behind Martin. Reluctantly, Michael, too, peered into the dark.

"I did hear something, I tell ya. Is anyone here?" Martin called.

Silence.

"You're hearing things." It may be only watery stew they were serving, but Michael had an appetite.

"Is anyone here?" Martin tried again.

Charlie kicked the inside of the crate.

"There," said Martin.

"It's a rat. Come on," Michael made for the steps.

"Hello." Charlie spoke out, but softly. His throat hurt and it was hard to yell over the noise of the ship's engine. "Hello," Charlie tried again.

"Jeeze, there is someone in there. Michael, get back here," Martin stuck his head through the hatch and yelled up the stairs.

Michael flew back down the steps. "You sure?"

"Hold the light. It came from one of those crates. Hello?

Hello? Where are you?"

"I'm here," said Charlie.

"You're right." Michael grabbed the ax that hung beside the door. "Which one?"

"Whoever you are, keep talking," Martin called out into the dark.

"Hello," mumbled Charlie. He was near delirious.

"This one," Martin thumped the side of Charlie's crate. "Hang on in there," he yelled over the drone of the ship's engine. "Michael, grab hold." Michael dropped the ax and the two of them shifted the stone-heavy crates. "The ax," Martin yelled to Michael. Martin grabbed hold of the ax and gave the crate Charlie was in a whack. The ax dropped to the floor, and with four hands well used to hauling nets of fish, Martin and Michael tore off the wooden slats. The crate cracked opened and its contents spilled onto the floor like a Christmas cracker.

"It's a kid!" Michael leaped back.

"Boy, you OK?" Martin bent down and cradled Charlie's head.

"What a stink. Are you sure that kid's alive? He smells like he's gone bad." Michael threw down a tarp. "Here, lay him out on this."

The two, ever so gently, shifted Charlie onto it.

"He's breathing. That's something," said Martin. "The kid must have been in there for three bloody days. Can you speak, boy? What's your name?"

"Char. Char Will," mumbled Charlie.

"Did you get that?" Michael asked.

"Char-something." Martin spoke directly into Charlie's ear. "What's your name? Say it again."

"Charlie Wilcox," whispered Charlie.

"Well, Charlie Wilcox, it was a right stupid thing you did, packing yourself into that crate."

"Wilcox. I know that name," Michael shone the flashlight in Charlie's face. "Martin, didn't your father sail with a Captain Wilcox?"

"That he did. Charlie, who is your father? Wake up." Charlie nodded off.

"He needs water," said Martin. "Get me a canteen."

Michael dashed through the hatch.

"Charlie, is your father Captain Samuel Wilcox? Sam Wilcox." Martin spoke slowly and loudly.

Charlie nodded.

"Here's the water." Michael passed the canteen to Martin, who held it up to Charlie's lips.

It was no sooner down his throat, when it came back up. Water dribbled down Charlie's chin. Still, he was breathing regularly, and his color looked better.

"We have to report him," said Michael.

"Turning in a Wilcox. I don't much care for that," replied Martin.

"There's not much else you can do. Besides, we're not even sure if he really is Skipper Sam's kid," said Michael.

Three sharp whistles sounded from on deck.

"That's us. We have to go, Martin. We'll be missed." Michael tried to be patient, but by nature, he was anything but a patient person.

"I know," Martin answered. "But, it will make no difference if we report him now or later. Let me just think on it." Martin slipped Charlie's haversack under his head. He propped the canteen up beside Charlie and folded the tarp around him, pig-in-a-poke fashion.

"You stay put, all right, Charlie?" Martin whispered into his ear. "I'll be back with some food, and then we'll decide what to do. Hear me? Just stay put."

Martin and Michael disappeared through the hatch.

THINGS WERE SHIFTING on the deck above.

Charlie sat up. He was stiff and sore; every muscle had a separate complaint. He looked around, slowly, like a turtle might. The hatch door had been left ajar and a thin slice of light shone in. Charlie licked his lips. His tongue was thick, too thick for his bone-dry mouth. He tried to swallow. And what was that smell? His hand fell on something hard and cool. What was it? It was round and made of tin. A canteen! Charlie unscrewed the top. His two hands shook like the devil as he raised it to his mouth. Water came up his throat and spurted on the floor. His head was spinning. He felt sick. Again, he heard pounding from above. They'd be at the ice, thought Charlie. No other reason to start shifting stuff about up top. Charlie's hand landed on the splintered crate. How did he get out of the crate? He'd had a dream about voices talking to him. But it was a dream.

Never mind. The ship should be slowing down any time now. The captain would be scanning for seals and ice pans. He could just see it. The captain would have a glass pressed to his eye. Once the seals were spotted, men would be dropped off in teams under the command of a master watch. The ship would then move on and drop off another team, and so it would go until every man who could hunt was skipping over ice pans like children in a playground.

What next? Charlie tried to focus his thoughts. The seal pelts would be gathered into bloody piles. By late afternoon, all sealers' eyes would go to the horizon in search of the ship that was to pick them up for the night. It was a cold, miserable thing to be left stranded on an ice floe overnight. Men died that way. It's just how it was.

Charlie clutched hold of a crate and struggled to his feet. They were bandy and he crumpled back down into a heap.

"Jeeze, come on," he spoke out loud, pretending there was someone else encouraging him on. Up again, he stumbled toward the hatch. He gave it a shove. The light hit him like a knife in the eyes. "Ohooooo," Charlie let out a yelp and crouched down. It hurt, it hurt so bad. He blinked, and blinked, and blinked again. He cupped his hand over his eyes and lurched out of the hold. Where was he? Gripping the metal railing and taking it slowly, he stumbled up the metal steps until he reached the first landing. He heard two voices. Charlie flattened his back against the wall and listened. They were coming closer. He ducked into a hatch directly behind him and tried not to breathe. Around him, bunks made of rough wood ran floor to top, four on one side, six on the other. Each bunk was fitted with thin green blankets. Great haversacks dangled from the walls like brown carcasses.

"Great day on the salt water, hu?" said the first voice.

"What say, we jig a few fish?" said the second voice. They passed by. Only their laughter lingered.

Charlie poked out his head. All clear. He started down the passage.

Dodging voices and the echo of boots clambering along the decks, Charlie made for the prow of the ship. He gripped the handle of a hatch door and pushed. Fresh air smacked him in the head. He took a long, deep breath. Sweet, salty air went into his lungs. Oh, Jeeze, but it felt good.

Charlie put his face into the wind and soaked it up like water. A mean wind blew away the sounds of the ship and there he stood, at the prow, looking out to sea. Blue, blue as far as the eye could see. Charlie closed his eyes and let the wind wash over him.

Blue? Blue? Charlie's eyes popped open. A blue sea! It's not supposed to be blue. Where was the ice? There was no ice. Not in front of him, not port, not starboard!

"Fall in."

Charlie turned round, slowly. Very slowly.

There, lying on the decks below, in various poses, some smoking, some nodding off, a few playing cards, others just milling about, were — soldiers. Hundreds of them.

"Boy!" A small man with the voice of two, pointed a long arm at Charlie. "You, boy."

"MOTHER'S MILK," grinned the battalion commanding officer, the C.O. they called him. He took two steady gulps from a silver-plated flask that seemed surgically attached to his hand. "Boy, do you know where we are headed?"

"No, sir."

"You hear that, Mister Horwood? Our young stowaway doesn't know where he's headed."

Horwood, the commander's batman, smirked. He would

have covered his nose, too, had it not been for the C.O. The stench of the kid was unbelievable.

"You must have boarded this ship for a reason, boy. What was it?"

It was a state of shock that Charlie was in. He tried to speak but all that came were squeaks. "To, to . . ."

"To, to . . . to the football field?" mocked the C.O. "What you think on that, Mister Horwood? Think the boy was on his way to play football and took a wrong turn maybe?"

"To the ice, sir." Charlie spoke. The words exploded out of his mouth.

"The ice!" The commander thumped his bulging stomach and laughed heartily. "Hear that, Mister Horwood? We have a sealer in our midst. The ice!" A snort from the flask calmed him down a bit.

"Looks to me like you got yourself on the wrong ship. You're going to war, boy. War! What do you think of that?"

Charlie's legs near buckled under him. War?

"How old are you, boy?"

War?

"Are you deaf? I said, how old are you?"

"Fourteen, coming on to fifteen, sir."

"Well, you're as good a man now as you're ever likely to be. What say we sign you up on the spot, hu?" The C.O. shot back another slug of spirits.

"My mother . . ." The lump in Charlie's throat threatened to suffocate him.

"Your mother? What's this about your mother? Do stowaways have mothers?"

"Yes, sir. It's just that my mother worries and, my

father . . ."

"Well, seems to me you should have thought on that before you decided to see the world. You're a long way from home now, boy. What shall we do with him, Mister Horwood?"

"Toss him overboard, sir." Mister Horwood pursed his ruby lips. He did nothing to hide his contempt for the situation. Sniveling, smelly boys were not his department.

"Seems a shame, though. Maybe we can get some work out of him first. Can you cook, boy?" asked the C.O.

"No, sir."

"Perfect. Take him to the galley, Mister Horwood," laughed the C.O. "Oh, and Mister Horwood, you might want to run a bit of water over the boy first. He seems a bit ripe to me."

Chapter 13

"My father sailed on the *Thetis*," said Martin proudly. "And it was your own father who captained her. My father said that a finer captain never sailed out of Brigus harbor than Captain Samuel Wilcox."

Just the mention of his father's name made Charlie feel sick inside. It was an ache in the pit of his stomach.

Martin and Charlie stood on deck looking out to a white-capped sea. The stench of unwashed bodies, stale cigs, overflowing latrines, and bloody awful food sent them topside whenever they could. Tucked under Charlie's arm was the spy glass. He was never far from it. It was his link to his home, to his father.

"Here," Martin offered Charlie a sip of smuggled rum.

The rum seared Charlie's tongue and near set his throat on fire.

"I thought it was a dream. I mean, when you got me out of the crate," said Charlie.

"If there was any dreaming it was me when I saw you walking down to the galley with that Horwood fellow," Martin laughed.

"No one knows — that you helped me," said Charlie, almost shyly.

"Good lad," Martin smiled back. He tossed back a shock of near white hair and looked out to where England was supposed to appear.

"My mother and father must be upset." Charlie's voice quivered.

"I have your letter here," Martin patted his pocket. "I'll put it in the company mail bag as soon as we land, Charlie. At least they'll know that you're not floundering on some ice floe."

Charlie thought on that. His mother would be crying, sure as anything. And what would his father be thinking? How would he feel about a son who made his mother cry? And what if he never came home again, never had a chance to say how sorry he was? And he was really, really sorry. He said as much in his letter.

"Dear Mother and Father," he wrote. "I didn't mean this to happen but I am on a ship bound for England. The soldiers are going on to Scotland for training. What's to become of me, I do not know yet. You must be very angry at me. I'm sorry. I am in good health and will try and get home as soon as I can. Your loving son, Charlie."

"Charlie-boy, snap out of it. You'll be home before ya

knows it and with a great adventure to tell, too," said Martin with a broad smile. "Think of what your pals will say when ya tell 'em that you sailed to England with the Newfoundland Regiment. Every kid at home will wish he was you."

"Do you think I should tell them that I spent three days in the crate, and the rest of the voyage peeling potatoes, or serving up a stew only fit for pigs?" muttered Charlie.

Martin threw his head back and laughed. "Naw, leave out that bit. Oh, Charlie, no worry. When we land in Blighty — that's what they call England — they'll just put you on a ship home. And that, Charlie-boy, will be the end of it. You may be home in time to read your own letter!"

Martin paused and looked up and down the ship. "Where is Michael? He'll want to catch the first glimpse of England."

Michael and Martin, both privates, trained for a summer in the St. John's Methodist Guards. Not yet twenty years old, they were fishermen all right. The two had spent three summers fishing down on the Labrador, and two seasons on the ice. The moment they stepped on this ship they had their sea legs, not like those poor beggars from the middle of Newfoundland. Had their heads hangin' over the rails "feeding the gulls" the minute the harbor was out of sight. Woodsmen.

As Martin was fair and a tall drink of water, Michael was dark and big. He had broad shoulders and hands like hammers. No two ways about it, Michael could be a contender, a boxer maybe, had he had the notion. Instead he was to join the Church after he had done his bit for God and country. He didn't speak much, which might not be a good thing for a minister. What Michael lacked in conversation, he made up for by playing his tin whistle almost constantly. It was tolerated, although a change of tune once in a while would have been welcomed. It was hymns he played, although they were hard to recognize.

Charlie liked Michael right enough, but it was Martin that he felt an instant kinship with. Martin was a protector by nature and choice. Not that the soldiers were mean to Charlie, just rowdy, excited like so many race horses just before the race. Bit prone to stupid comments. "Are we fighting with children?" was one. Harmless really.

"Leave him be," said Martin. And that would be the end of it.

"We'll be seeing the coast anytime," said Martin. They looked to where they hoped England would suddenly rear up like some mythical beast. "We'll be a long time in Scotland before we're sent to the front." Martin adjusted his tunic and gave the whole thing a proper yank. Martin was proud of his uniform. Proud to wear it and defend England, proud to fend off the murderous hordes of Huns that threatened civilization itself, but it was for the honor of Newfoundland that got his blood up. His puttees were wrapped smartly, starting just under his knee where his breeches ended. The buttons on his tunic gleamed like so many gold nuggets. Martin didn't wear a Sam Brown belt like the officers, but that would come soon. He didn't mean to stay a private for very long.

"Aren't you afraid?" Charlie asked.

"Afraid?" Martin was genuinely shocked. "I'm no sloucher."

"But what if you get killed?" Charlie stood, one foot on

the railing, his spy glass pressed up to his eye. He wanted to be the first to see land.

"I can't die," laughed Martin. "I made a promise to my girl." Martin pulled a tarnished cigarette case from the inside of his tunic and flipped it open with one hand. A little row of homemade cigarettes were lined up on one side of the case and on the other, a picture.

Martin passed the case to Charlie. A beautiful, young woman with a small smile and dark hair tumbled on top of her head looked back at him.

"She's pretty," said Charlie as he passed the case back to Martin. "What's her name?"

"Meeta. She's the prettiest girl in all of Newfoundland, I'll wager." Martin gazed at the picture. He traced her face, and hair, with his finger before snapping the case shut and tucking it back into the pocket of his tunic. "You got a girl?"

Charlie thought of Claire.

"No."

"Have ya ever been in love?" Martin grinned.

"No." Charlie's face went pink. But he thought of Mac and wondered if he had. Charlie brought the spy glass to his eye and scanned the horizon.

"Well, I tell you, when ya fall in love with a girl like my Meeta, you're not about to go and get yourself killed. We're to get married as soon as I get back. Before long, I'll have a boat of my own, kids to feed, but, well, a man's got to have a little adventure before he settles into it, ya know. Just hope the war ain't all over before we get there."

Martin took long drags from his cigarette while Charlie peered through his glass.

"There was somebody," Charlie said shyly. "That I liked . . . as a friend."

"Ah, you rogue. You was holding out."

"No, it wasn't like that." Charlie passed pink altogether and went straight to crimson. Even his ears were hot.

"There's a nurse, and she's somewhere, in France, or maybe England, and . . ."

And then the whole story came tumbling out of Charlie's mouth like nothing could stop it. How Mac had taken such good care of him in hospital. All about Davy. How he and Davy saw Mac and her doctor kissing on the roof. Then the shame crept over him — how he had told on them. Not meaning to, mind, just blabbing like a fool before he was put under anesthetic. Doctors and nurses weren't allowed to fall in love. He got them canned. Now, because of his loose tongue, they joined up and could get themselves killed. All on account of him.

Charlie touched his pocket, and for a moment he thought he might show Martin Mac's picture, the one Davy drew. But, no.

Martin thought on Charlie's story a bit. He might have laughed. It wasn't hard to tell that Charlie was in love with this nurse after all, Martin was not long out of fourteen himself.

"Charlie," Martin spoke slowly, like he had a point to make. "You said that when you woke up from the operation, they were right there, Mac and the doctor. They were in uniform."

"Yep, right there. They had come to say good-bye to me, before leaving for war." Charlie again lifted the spy glass to his eye.

"Well ol' boy, it takes more than a day to sign up and . . ."

"There!" squealed Charlie.

"Land ho," hollered a voice from above. England was off the port bow. A thin sliver of land to be sure, but England it was. As the ship drew closer, they could see the startling great white cliffs of chalk, mountain high, welcoming them.

"Look at it, Martin, the white cliffs of Dover."

"At last," said Martin. "London's not far now. Then the fun begins."

Chapter 14

"*S*ir." Charlie stood directly in front of the C.O. They were surrounded by hundreds of soldiers, all standing in a giant, makeshift shed on the dock. It was all kitbags, haversacks, and uniforms. Soldiers by the hundreds jostled for air. You could near taste the thrill of events to come. From above, it looked like a hive of brown beetles scurrying from pillar to post for no good reason. Hanging from the rafters were the flags of the Allies, most of which Charlie didn't recognize. The biggest of all was the Union Jack. And pinned to the walls were posters of a rather fierce-looking fellow, Lord Kitchener maybe, the British War Minister. He pointed a long arm from a poster and told them all to join up. Well they had joined up, hadn't they?

"Move off," hollered the C.O. "Make way." He looked

down at Charlie. "Ah, the stowaway. The one on his way to play football. Well, you're in for a helluva game now, boy."

"Sir, where should I go?" asked Charlie.

"I have better things to do, boy. Talk to Mister Horwood." The C.O. turned away and rattled his silver-top ash stick in the air. "Make way, make way," he hollered. A path was made, and like Moses crossing the Dead Sea, the C.O. moved through the masses.

"Charlie. Charlieeee."

It was Martin's disembodied voice. But Martin was nowhere to be seen.

"Martin!" Charlie leaped up, hollered back, and leaped up again. "I'm here, I'm here." Even if Martin was standing on Charlie's foot, Charlie might have not seen him.

"Charlie!" Martin tried again.

"Here. Here!" And then whack, Charlie got a kitbag in the face.

"Hey, watch it." Charlie pushed back but shoved the wrong guy. "Oh, sorry."

"Charlie!" Martin emerged from the mass of men, all huffs and puffs, his white hair sticking out from under his cap. There was a smile plastered on his face that could reach back to Newfoundland. "Exciting, isn't it, Charlie? Are you OK? Are they sending you home?" The crowd swayed and Charlie was near knocked off his feet.

"I'll be fine. Good luck, Martin," said Charlie. He reached out to Martin but two soldiers suddenly came between them.

"It's the great adventure that I'm on, Charlie. Now get you to your home. Promise me. Get home. You'll be all right then . . ."

"Martin . . ."

A shout came from somewhere. "Fall in." Martin was swallowed up. The soldiers all seemed to magically find their place and order emerged. In the distance a band played and women in large black hats, holding the hands of small children, stood behind a rope and waved.

Mister Horwood, whose responsibilities included polishing the C.O.'s boots and buttons, walked calmly down the gangplank, avoiding the rabble and confusion at all costs. Men in hordes were disgusting creatures. Smelly, too. Mister Horwood dabbed his bow-tie lips with his handkerchief as he skirted the crowd.

Charlie scrambled over haversacks, through legs, and over two boxes to set himself in front of the man.

"Mister Horwood, it's me, Charlie Wilcox."

"So I see. I thought I had given instructions to have you tossed overboard." Mister Horwood sniffed and cast his eyes outward. A bath and glass of brandy would go down nicely right about now.

"Sir, I'm to find a ship home, and . . ."

"Boy, do I look like a ship home? Is there anything about me that resembles a ship? Do you see a smokestack coming out of my head? Is there a rudder trailing behind me that I am unaware of?"

"No, sir, I mean . . ."

"Against my better judgment," Mister Horwood huffed, "I was ordered to make some arrangements for you. A telegram has been sent to the Newfoundland Regiment office. Your parents will be contacted in due course and asked for restitution for your passage — both ways!" Mister Horwood smiled. "Do you know what *restitution* means, boy?" The smile turned into a broad-tooth grin.

Charlie shook his head.

"It means they will have to pay to get you back, assuming they want you back. Once the paperwork is done, I assume you will be sent home."

"Thank you." Charlie was grateful, really. He looked past Mister Horwood to the soldiers. It was exciting. It would be over long before he was old enough to fight.

"Boy," Mister Horwood boomed, "pay attention. You will report to the quartermaster's office in eight weeks. That's not to say you'll get passage home."

"Eight weeks!" The blood all but drained out of Charlie's face. "What am I to do until then?"

"Well," drooled Mister Horwood, "unless you plan to starve, might I suggest you get a job? Then again, you could turn petty thief, get arrested, and spend your time in a British brig. Might that suit you?" (It was not a question that required an answer.) "Whatever your plans are, it's no business of mine. Now — go away." But it was Mister Horwood who went away. Charlie stood rooted to the spot.

In no time the shed was empty. On the heels of the soldiers tromped a marching band, and behind it, a gaggle of cheering women and children.

Now what? Charlie brushed his hair from his forehead until it stood up in sweaty points. Home was thousands of miles away. And between him and it, an ocean. And no one at home knew yet. "I'm sorry, Mother," he mumbled.

Charlie shuffled down through the shed and onto the pier. He hoisted himself up on a shaky, wooden barrier and looked out to the ocean. "How could I have done this?" Now that there was no one to see, the tears rose up and ran down his face. "Please," Charlie mouthed the words to the sky, "I want to go home."

"Boy, could I get some help, please?"

A nurse, her stiff, white veil pinned primly to her head, tapped Charlie on the shoulder. Charlie cleaned up his face with the back of his sleeve.

"I am looking for the boat that will take me across the Channel to France," she said, taking no notice of Charlie's tearful state. "Could you direct me?"

"I don't know. But I could carry your bags," said Charlie. It's not like he had anything better to do. Besides, she had two valises and a shoulder bag.

"You're not English, are you?" said the nurse.

"No, ma'am. I'm from Newfoundland. But I can carry just as good as any Englishman."

"Newfoundland," she sniffed. "That's in Canada, isn't it?"

"No, ma'am. We're part of the British Empire." Charlie would have gone on and told the part of being a self-government dominion just like he was taught in Miss Rabbitt's grade four class, but one tug of the valise took his breath away. Jeeze, Charlie thought, what was in here — bricks?

"Medical supplies." She read Charlie's grimace on his face. "What is your name?"

"Charlie Wilcox," he huffed as he tried to keep up.

"Well, Charlie Wilcox, my name is Ellen. I am off to Boulonge and then to Etaples. Walk smartly, boy. The soldiers call it Eat Apples." Ellen laughed like a horse, in snorts. "There are twelve hospitals there, almost 2,600 beds." Ellen marched as she talked, really marched!

"Are there Newfoundland doctors and nurses there, too?" Charlie, huffing, suddenly brightened up.

"I expect so. Where the Newfoundland Regiment goes, their own medical corps are sure to follow — lambs at the slaughter, wouldn't you say?" Ellen sucked back air, then snorted it out in a big blast of laughter. "And I do believe, not sure, mind you, that they are connected with the Canadian medical corps. The Canadians are in Etaples in great numbers. Now tell me, where are you off to?"

Without so much as a pause, Charlie said, "To Etaples."

Chapter 15

*N*urse Ellen's valises weren't getting any lighter.

"Wait," groaned Charlie. "I'll get a trolley."

A derelict old trolley, pushed off to the side, was brought into action. The valises were piled high, and Ellen topped the load with her great coat. A Red Cross armband circled the arm of the coat.

Off they went, through the shed and onto yet another pier and another shed. Colorful flags were everywhere, along with Red Cross collection boxes, recruiting posters, and advertisements for all sorts of things, including Horlick's Malted Milk Tablets — whatever they were.

"Here we are," said Ellen. She plucked her bags from the trolley like they were featherweights.

Papers were shown at the bottom of the gangplank. Ellen handed Charlie a coin, which he was about to give back, but then he thought better of it and slipped it in his pocket. She tromped up to the ship and didn't so much as nod good-bye.

Ah, well. Charlie smiled as he reached into his pocket, and smiled some more when he pulled out the Red Cross armband — the one that had been around the arm of Ellen's coat. Ducking into the shadows, Charlie wrapped it around his own arm and walked to the back of the pier to wait. It didn't take long.

"Can I carry your bags?" Charlie faced a young British nurse, also wearing a Red Cross armband.

"How kind. Thank you."

With his head near tucked under his arm, Charlie trailed the nurse up the gangplank onto an old steamer. It was a rust bucket, that was sure, but so far, so good.

"Thank you again," said the nurse.

Charlie parked the bags at the top of the gangplank, gave the nurse a nod, and bolted down to the hold of the boat. Best not to chance an inspection. He knew where the hold was. Ships were all alike that way.

THE CROSSING FROM ENGLAND to Calais, France, took three hours or more. Disembarking was easy; everything on the dock was a muddle. Soldiers back from leave or hospital, nurses and support staff, lorries, wagons, mules, refugees, soldiers, and horses milled about.

"How do I get to Etaples?" Charlie asked a young soldier.

"Follow them," he said, as if his words cost money.

Charlie trailed behind a line of medical personnel and boarded the train. He made himself small. The fewer questions asked of him, the better. An hour later, there it was — Etaples.

It was a war-weary town. The cobbled streets and wounded buildings looked lifeless. A church spire leaned at an angle, and the front of the building was ripped off. It was like looking into his sisters' dollhouse after the dog had gotten into it.

All the medical types, and a trail of boxes carried on men's shoulders, were going in one direction. Charlie stumbled behind, head down, and boarded a British double-decker bus. It would have been fun had the windows not been boarded up. A couple of soldiers were ringing the bell and asking to get off at Golders Green, a place that Charlie thought must be in England.

Ten minutes later, on the outskirts of the town of Etaples, the bus stopped. And there it was, a sight that took his breath away.

A hospital city made up of hundreds of faded, cream-colored tents stretched for ten miles or more. There were some buildings, of course, the type hammered together in a day, temporary by any standards. And in the middle of this hospital city stood a chateau, one that had seen better days. The bus emptied and Charlie stood and looked around.

"Excuse me," Charlie spoke to a nurse in a gray coat trimmed with a red collar. "I'm looking for the Newfoundland hospital?"

"Everything in these parts is Australian," said the nurse.

"Go on up to the Canadian area and ask there. Stay on this road until you pass the quarry. The nurses' hostel is on the left, and the chateau is on the other side. You'll come to the Canadian and Red Cross hospitals, just down from the cemetery."

Charlie trudged along, passing tent after tent. The walk took the better part of the afternoon. At last, the Canadian area. A Red Cross flag, along with the ensign, flapped outside many of the tents. Two nurses, both walking at a brisk clip, passed him, too. They were Canadians, easy to tell since they had "Canada" embroidered on the shoulders of their gray-blue skirt and blouse uniforms.

"Ahhh, excuse . . ." But they were gone.

A local boy wearing a beret and carrying two obviously heavy water pails near knocked him down. This time Charlie held his ground.

"Hey!" Charlie yelled and then ran after him. "Where is the Newfoundland hospital?"

'No English, no English," said the boy while puffing.

"Excuse me, nurse." Charlie, totally exasperated, stood at the entrance to what looked like a main tent. "Is this the Newfoundland Regiment hospital?"

"Sister."

"Pardon?"

"You call the nurses here 'sister,' not nurse." The nurse, or rather sister, walked on by. It took more than a few broad strides to catch up to her.

"I am looking for Lily MacKenzie, she's a nurse from Newfoundland," said Charlie.

"Never heard of her," was the clip reply, and away she went.

"Excuse me," Charlie asked yet another nurse, rather *sister*. "Do you know a sister from Newfoundland named Lily MacKenzie?"

"I do not, and who would be asking?" The sister stopped and glared down at Charlie. "You're a bit young for this, aren't you?" She motioned to the Red Cross armband on Charlie's arm.

"No, ma'am. I'm a volunteer."

The sister sniffed. "Well, best check in with Matron. We can use someone to sweep the floors — or are you a doctor?" It wasn't really a question. The sister went off, chuckling.

Charlie tossed his haversack down and plunked himself down beside it. This was useless. How would he ever find Mac? He was tired and hungry and cold. Spring had just arrived and with it a dampness that went to the bone.

"What are you doing sitting there?"

Startled, Charlie looked up, looked way up. He looked past the spit-shiny black boots, the pristine white uniform that encased a battleship of a body, all the way up to the steely, silver-rimmed glasses. Visions of Nurse Butters sprang to his mind.

"I'm here to . . ." Charlie scrambled to his feet, ". . . to help, ma'am."

"What can the likes of you do to help? Are you a spy?"

A spy? Charlie was shocked. "No, ma'am. I'm an order-ly." Charlie dithered a bit.

"Every medical person in this unit is trained, boy," said the woman. "We're not the British, you know. We don't take every passing warm body and put them in a medical uniform."

"No, ma'am. I just meant that I could . . . sweep and . . ."
Charlie was at a loss. He looked around at the city of tents.
The only thing that seemed real at that very moment was
the grumble in his stomach.

"You're hungry, aren't you?" If she was softening toward
him, Charlie couldn't tell by her voice.

"Yes, ma'am."

"We'll have no laggards. If you want to eat, then you'll
have to work for it. See that tent?" She pointed to one of
the larger tents. "That's a dressing station. You know what
that is, boy?"

"Charlie, ma'am."

"Pardon?"

"My name is Charlie Wilcox, ma'am. And a dressing
station is where you sort out the wounded." It was a guess,
and a good one.

The sister gave him a long, steady look and then said,
"Well, you are smarter than you look. Go in there, Charlie
Wilcox, and tell the sister there that I sent you." The sister
turned to leave.

"Excuse me . . . ah," Charlie said.

"Are you addressing me?"

"Yes, ma'am. Who are you?" Charlie asked.

"I am the Matron-in-Chief, and that is how you will
address me."

And Matron-in-Chief walked away.

Charlie stumbled over to the tent. A water barrel,
covered by a mirror-thin coat of ice, stood at the entrance.
Charlie took a ladle off the hook and plunged it through
the ice. It cracked like glass and split into a thousand little
ice pans floating in the sea. He scooped up the water and

drank. Better. He felt much better.

Charlie walked inside the tent and stopped dead. Laid out in front of him on spindly wooden cots on a floor of wooden planks were dozens of wounded men huddled under thin, gray blankets. Some had their legs bound up, others their arms. Some had their whole heads wrapped in cotton with holes sticking out where their noses were supposed to be.

It was a cold, damp, miserable place. Their breath hung in the air like tissue-thin cotton balls, which was reassuring. Only live men could breathe.

Charlie walked down the row, slowly, not knowing where to look or what to do. At the center of the tent was a stove and on the top of the stove, a black cast-iron kettle. The sickest were clustered around the stove, taking what little warmth was in the offering. A sister looked up from a desk.

"Yes," she said, and kindly.

"I'm here . . . Matron-in-Chief sent me . . . to help."

Chapter 16

"*I* am glad to hear that you have been working for your keep." Matron-in-Chief sat primly behind a huge mahogany desk. It was said that it took six men, and a horse, to fetch the desk from the chateau at her request, or rather, demand.

"Yes, ma'am." Charlie drew his shoulders back and stood at attention. Everyone stood at attention in Matron-in-Chief's presence, even the General.

"Sister reports that you have done well," Matron-in-Chief peered down at the papers before her. "Now it seems that it will be sometime before you will get passage home. Apparently your parents have been contacted and are willing to pay for your ticket. You will go back to London to wait for your papers. Dismissed."

But Charlie didn't leave. Not a'tall. He stood there like his boots were nailed to the floor.

"Ma'am?"

"Dismissed," Matron-in-Chief barked again without so much as casting up an eyebrow (she only had one).

"Ma'am, if I'm not to get passage home for some time, what would I be doing in London?"

"That is none of my concern, now . . ."

"What I mean to say is, if it's all the same to you, I might as well stay here until I get my ticket home."

"This is a hospital, young man, not a school yard."

"Yes, ma'am, but I am fourteen, only a few years younger than these soldiers. And I am a Newfoundlander, too, and you said yourself that I've done good work so far, and, well, going home seems — cowardly." There, he said it. He was not a coward, and if God himself had seen fit to drop him in this spot, well, made sense that he was to do his bit right alongside everyone else. Leastways that's how Charlie reasoned it out — even if there was no reasoning to be had. "What I mean to say is," Charlie rushed on, "I know how you like things. It's hard to keep the place clean and orderly, like at home."

Charlie touched a nerve and he knew it.

"Indeed it is." Matron-in-Chief rose up from her chair. "These army doctors don't understand that a hospital runs on cleanliness, order, and discipline." Matron-in-Chief thumped her desk.

"Yes, ma'am. And I could help, I mean, until I get my passage home."

Matron-in-Chief hesitated a bit, which was unusual, before slapping her fist down on her desk. "We are short of orderlies, very short indeed. Very well, consider yourself an official volunteer. You may continue on with your present duties. I'll talk to Sister about getting you a uniform. How about your quarters — are they sufficient?"

Charlie might have replied that one wool blanket, a cot, and a space in the broom closet were not really quarters but instead he said, "They are fine, ma'am."

"Good. Dismissed."

DAYS TURNED INTO WEEKS. If Charlie's papers had fallen between the cracks of army bureaucracy, no one seemed to notice or care, least of all Charlie. Not that he didn't think about his parents — he did, every day, every hour of the day. He had sent a letter, of course, but had no way of knowing if it got there or not. If he could just talk to them, tell them not to worry, that he was doing his bit.

There wasn't much time to think. Besides washing floors, washing everything, rolling bandages, and changing blankets, Charlie ran errands. There was a slight money problem, but that was easily solved. In exchange for tracking down cigs, and the occasional bottle of whisky, he got tips. The cash came in handy given that he wasn't on any payroll.

"Psssst, hey, boy," a soldier laid out on a stretcher motioned to Charlie. "Get me some cigs, will ya?"

"Yea, got some right here." Charlie searched his pockets before coming up with four homemade, slightly worn, cigarettes. The soldier fished out a few francs from a haversack under his cot.

"Do me a favor there, kid, help me up. I'd like to sit

outside," said the soldier.

Charlie slid his arm under the soldier and the two hobbled to a wooden fold-up chair just outside the tent. An ambulance lorry emptied another batch of wounded right in front of them. Neither of them paid it much mind.

"Yer a Newfoundlander like myself, I expect," said the soldier.

"I am," replied Charlie.

"It's a grand day for jigging, ain't it, boy?" the soldier said sadly as he looked up to the summer sky. "You a townie?"

Charlie shook his head. "I'm from Brigus."

"Ah, a bayman," the soldier took a drag. "What are we doing so far from home, I wonder. What's this all about, hu?" The soldier gave up a weak smile while sucking on his cig.

Charlie picked up a broom.

It was a grand day. That was always the strangest part — how a day could be so beautiful, and yet, not so far away, men who had never met were deliberately trying to kill each other. And somewhere, on this same earth, Jim Norton was running off to fish or swim, Claire was picking berries up on Grave Hill, and his own parents may be sitting down to dinner. The moment Charlie thought of his parents a wave of guilt, and something like hunger, came over him. It left him breathless.

Then he saw her.

"I am to report to Matron-in-Chief. Which way?" Mac, Sister Lily MacKenzie, climbed out of the back of the ambulance and looked Charlie square in the face. She was tired, bone tired. Charlie dropped his broom.

"Mac?"

"Pardon me?" said Mac.

"Lily, Mac, I mean Lily, it's me, Charlie."

"I'm sorry, I . . ."

"Charlie Wilcox, from Newfoundland. It's me, Mac — Charlie!"

The suitcase fell to the ground and almost before the thud, Charlie felt Mac's arms wrap around him.

"Charlie. No, it can't be. Charlie?" It didn't make sense. "Let me look at you." Mac cupped her hands over Charlie's ears and stared into his eyes. "It is you." And she hugged him again. This time Charlie hugged back.

"How is your foot? Why are you here?" Mac cried.

"I came to . . . I was on a ship to the ice. Never mind." It all sounded too stupid for words. Charlie hardly believed it, how could Mac?

"Sister MacKenzie, I presume." Matron-in-Chief came around the bend and spat out Mac's name like it was bad meat — but Matron always talked that way. "You are three hours late."

"Yes, Matron-in-Chief, we were delayed." Mac straightened up so fast she near split something. Charlie tucked his chin, and his grin, into his shirt.

"There is a war on, but punctuality still counts, MacKenzie. I see you two know each other. Very well. Charlie, take MacKenzie to the nurses' hostel." And to Mac she said, "Have a cup of tea, and then report for duty." Matron turned on her heels and marched off.

"Remind you of anyone?" Charlie smiled.

"The ghost of Nurse Butters," and the two burst out laughing.

"The nurses' hostel is a long way," Charlie said. "Are you

up for the walk?"

"I suddenly feel like a new person. I could walk beside you all day."

If it was possible to die of happiness, Charlie would have expired on the spot.

SEVERAL WEEKS PASSED. While the nights were chilly, the early summer days were sunny and warm. The rumble of the distant guns, and the constant arrival of wounded, kept them all working twelve, sometimes fifteen hours a day. But the war itself seemed unreal. Oh, the wounded were real enough, but the actual fighting, well, it was hard to fathom. He heard the stories right enough, but still . . .

Charlie's duties increased to binding wounds and changing dressings. No one questioned Charlie's age anymore, or what he was doing there.

The news came on a sunny day. Mac was sitting on a chair beside a soldier's cot when she saw Charlie coming down the row with his arms full of folded bandages.

"Charlie," she whispered. She untangled her hand from the wounded soldier's grip. "Meet me outside."

Charlie nodded and glanced down at the soldier. He wouldn't last the night. Charlie could tell these things now. He put the bandages on a trolley and followed Mac down the row of beds and out into the open air.

"A letter came for you today." Mac pulled an envelope out from her pocket. The envelope was addressed to Mac, but in the corner was Charlie's name.

"It's from my father!" Charlie ripped the envelope open.

A ten pound note fell out. A fortune! Charlie grinned and slipped it into his pocket.

Dear Charlie,

We received your last letter. Your mother and I are glad to hear that you are safe and nowhere near the front. I have been down to St. John's Regimental office many times. As you can imagine, getting passage home is difficult, but not impossible. It's taken a lot longer than we first thought. There is a troop ship, the SS Bonavista, leaving England mid-afternoon on July 2. We have secured you a passage.

It's paid in full. You are to make your way to England as soon as possible. Check with the quartermaster. He will have your ticket. Charlie, remember, July 2. The ship sails at noon. This chance won't come along again.

We miss you, son. Your mother is better. The influenza took a great deal out of her, but she's up and about now. Worry about yourself, Charlie, and come home safe.

Your loving father,
Samuel Wilcox

"Is everything OK Charlie?" Mac put her hand on his shoulder.

"My mom was sick and I didn't even know about it," Charlie said sadly.

"Never mind, you'll be with them soon." Mac smiled at him.

Charlie felt her smile inside himself, and it hurt.

"They have found a way for me to get home," he whispered.

"Charlie," Mac threw her arms around him, near knocking him down in the process. "That's wonderful."

"Yes, I guess."

"When are you to sail?"

"A week from now, July 2, from England." Charlie folded the letter and put it in his pocket. "Mac, would you come somewhere with me? I mean . . ." Charlie fumbled for words. "I mean, I want to take you somewhere."

"Charlie, I'm in the middle of my shift."

"After. I mean . . ." This was bloody hard. "I want to take you to a place after your shift."

"A place? Charlie, what are you talking about?"

Charlie's heart thumped. "Just meet me in front of the nurses' hostel, OK?"

As if he was afraid she might say no, Charlie jumped up, spun on his heels, and bolted.

Chapter 17

"*Madame*," Charlie stood in one of the last bakery shops in Etaples. Although it was more like a gloomy hovel than a proper shop.

"*Avez-vous la pain?*" Charlie spoke slowly and loudly.

"*Non, Monsieur. Pas de lapin,*" replied the snarly, and very cross, shopkeeper.

Charlie looked at the loaves of bread lined up behind the counter.

"*Une la pain, une la pain,*" repeated Charlie. Well, this was frustrating.

"*Non, Monsieur,*" said the woman, her hands waving in frustration. "*Pas de lapin.*"

"Ack, are ya having a wee bit of trouble, boy?" A big,

corpulent Irishman from the Ulster Division burst into the shop.

"She won't sell me a loaf of bread!" said Charlie. "I keep asking her for *la pain*, and she says she has none, but look." Charlie pointed to the bread.

"Well, it could be that she doesn't like the look of ya," the Ulsterman said slowly, "or it could be that she really does not have a rabbit." His laughter ricocheted around the little shop. "*Lapin* means rabbit," the Ulsterman sucked in needed air, "*du pain* is bread." And he started laughing all over again.

"Well, I've not much need for French in Newfoundland," Charlie was put out.

"*Madame*," said the Ulsterman to the shopkeeper, "*Pourriez-vous donner du bon pain français à notre petit ami anglais?*"

"*Aah, du pain!*" the shopkeeper flung a loaf of bread into Charlie's arms.

"Ask her for some cheese too," said Charlie.

The Ulsterman smiled again and said, "*Et il paraît qui'il veut un morceau du fromage aussi.*"

"And that basket," Charlie pointed to a wicker basket behind the counter.

The Ulsterman grinned. "*Et ce panier-là.*"

"*Le panier?*" the shopkeeper held the basket high.

"*Oui, celui-ci. Figurez-vous que notre petit ami a l'intention de fixer un rendez-vous?*"

The Ulsterman eyed Charlie and roared with laughter. Even the shopkeeper smirked.

"What are you two laughing at? What are you saying?" Charlie was indignant.

"You're planning something here, sure aren't ya, boy?"
The soldier shifted his own bag.

Charlie scowled at the two, emptied his pockets, and
held his palm out flat. The shopkeeper picked through his
francs.

"Planning what? Yea, I'm planning to eat." Charlie was
now mortified. Nothing could stop his cheeks from turning into two red fireballs.

"Ach, sure," said the soldier, and to the shopkeeper he
said, "*Seulement une baguette pour moi.*" The solider, still
grinning, paid for his own loaf of bread.

"*Bonne chance!*" The shopkeeper pointed at Charlie
and cackled.

Charlie grumbled under his breath.

With the goods tucked into the picnic basket, Charlie
followed the soldier out of the shop.

"Ah, wait up. Do you have wine in that bag?" Charlie
asked, as they picked their way down the muddy road.

"That I do, boy."

"Could I buy a bottle?"

"Now, what would a wee lad like yourself be doing with
a bottle of wine?"

Charlie pointed to the Red Cross badge on his arm.
"Watch it. You might be needing me one day." Which set
the Ulsterman off into another fit of laughter. There was
nothing, it seemed, that didn't make this fellow laugh.

"Aye, it would be a good thing to have a medical man
like yourself onside."

"One English pound," said Charlie, looking him
square in the eyes. It was a bloody good offer and they both
knew it.

"Sold." And the Ulsterman handed over a bottle, one of many.

Charlie thanked his father for the money under his breath.

"And how da ya plan to open it?"

Open it? Charlie looked down at the corked bottle.

"Here," the Ulsterman laughed hardy and tossed him a corkscrew, which was no more than a screw hammered through a block of wood. "Good luck." And to himself, "Sure you'll be needing it."

Charlie leaped onto a passing flatbed army lorry and headed back to hospital grounds. In no time, he was at the door of the nurses' hostel. He ran his fingers through his hair. It would not stay down. He looked at the mud on his boots. What a mess. Standing on one foot, he gave the other foot a shine by rubbing the boot on the back of his pants. A hop, and the other foot got the works, too. It didn't work. His boots were still dirty and now so were his pants.

Basket in hand, he waited and waited. A sister and an enlisted man on crutches passed by. Well what were they grinning at?

He looked down at the booty. Not bad, he thought. Cheese, bread, wine. Oh no. He could have smacked himself in the head. A blanket. You couldn't have a picnic without a blanket to sit on! Right.

Charlie skirted the nurses' hostel, ditched the basket under the steps, and snuck in the back door. Where would they keep the blankets? The laundry. All laundry rooms were in the basement. Down he went, taking the stairs two at a time. Sure enough, a stack of thin gray blankets were neatly piled just inside the laundry room. He nabbed one.

"Hey, you," yelled some disembodied voice from behind a series of porcelain tubs. Too late. Charlie was back up the stairs, three at a time.

On the way up, he passed a tea tray that sat on a little table on the landing. He snatched two blue-rimmed china cups. He kept going. "Where are you going with those?" hollered yet another voice.

"Thank you," Charlie whispered. He raced out the back door of the hostel, grabbed the basket, charged around to the front, and . . . there she was.

"Charlie!" Lily looked at a puffed-out Charlie, the basket, the wine, the blanket. She was astonished and there was no denying it.

"Hi." Charlie coughed.

"Wine, Charlie?" Mac pointed to the bottle poking out from the basket. "Should you be drinking wine?"

"Yes, no, yes." He tried to catch his breath and sputter all at the same time.

"I'm sorry, Charlie, you've gone to a lot of trouble. I can't think why I even said that. If you're old enough to watch good men die, I guess you're old enough to drink wine. Let's start again. Where are we off to?" Mac smiled.

"It's a place I found. It's over the bridge, on the bank of the river. It's . . . it's like the sea, if you pretend. It's like home." Even in the dusk Charlie couldn't hide his pink face.

"Then let's go." Mac turned and walked a few steps ahead of him. Charlie couldn't take his eyes off of her. Wisps of blonde hair had escaped her nurse's veil. She was bundled in a long gray cape, over an ankle-length blue dress. On her sleeves were pristine white cuffs, "leg-o'-mutton" sleeves they called them. There was no sign of her apron, the one with the giant Red Cross on the front. If she was dressed in a gold silk gown, with a tiara sitting where her veil was, she couldn't have looked more beautiful to Charlie.

Charlie tried to focus his eyes straight ahead.

The two picked their way through the ruts in the road. The mud under their feet was both hard and slippery at the same time, like a scum coating solid ground. Once or twice Mac reached out and took hold of Charlie's arm. It was like they were walking out together.

They crossed the bridge that spanned the River Canche, skirted the scrub pine, and ducked under the poplar trees. A little path opened up, and the mud under foot was replaced by soft woodland. And then a clearing, not too big.

"Here's the spot." Charlie dropped the basket and spread the blanket out on a rare patch of grass.

"It's wonderful here, Charlie. I'd forgotten how beautiful this country is."

Maybe, Charlie thought. What with the great, sweeping sand dunes by the sea and the lush, sloping farmland. But now towns and villages that had been in existence for hundreds and hundreds of years were heaps of rubble.

To one side they could see the tip of the hospital grounds. To the other side, and in the distance, were two doll-size farms. Most farmhouses were billets now, places for soldiers to stay — not for infantry men, of course, but for officers. Sometimes a farm wife stayed on and served the officers home-cooked dinners. Her husband and sons were off to war, maybe, or dead. Most of the local residents had packed up and left, refugees in their own country.

Charlie fumbled with the corkscrew. He was getting nowhere fast.

"Here, let me." Mac took over the task. Charlie held out two cups as Mac poured.

"Cheers. Charlie, this is good! Where on earth did you . . . Don't tell me." Mac took a second sip. "And bread and cheese — it's a feast!" The two tore off hunks of bread and broke off bits of cheese. "Everything is all mixed up, isn't it? You should be going to school and I should . . ." Mac's voice just faded away.

"What were you going to say?" Charlie's mouth was full.

"Oh, it sounds too simple now, too much of a dream. But if I was home now, who knows? Maybe I'd be living in a little house by the sea, and having my first baby." Mac looked out across the fields.

Standing in what passed as a hospital ward, after a twelve-hour shift, she was beautiful. But now, in this light, she could have been an angel. Not with a halo burning above her head — no, the sun came from inside her. It was as if, thought Charlie, she had swallowed a halo whole.

Charlie took a swig of wine. Truth be told, it tasted awful. Least the first and second sip did. Now the third gulp was going down just fine.

"Mac, I have to tell you something." Charlie looked straight ahead. "It's about when you signed up, you know, in St. John's."

"I've been meaning to apologize for that, Charlie," said Mac softly.

"Why?"

"I wanted to tell you days before your operation that we

had signed up, but we needed to keep it quiet until Robert had a chance to talk to his mother."

"Days? You, and Dr. Daniels, signed up days before my operation?" Charlie scrambled to put it together. "So, so I had nothing to do with — with your coming here?"

"Why no, Charlie. Why would you have thought that?"

"No reason, none at all." Charlie smiled.

"Charlie, what are you not telling me?" Lily turned and stared intently at him. Charlie gazed over the fields. He had an ironic smirk plastered over his face. Well, what do you know! He shook his head and smiled to himself all over again.

"Charlie! What are you laughing at!" Lily demanded.

"Nothing."

"Nothing? All right, I have a question for you. Why did you stow away on that ship in the first place?"

His smile vanished. He shrugged. The words, "not fit for the ice," came back to him like an echo.

"Charlie?"

"I wanted to . . ." What could he say? "I wanted to prove to my father that I was strong enough to go to the ice, to fish, to sail." There, he said it. The words hung in the air like laundry on a line. He felt foolish.

"I met your father, and your mother, when you were in hospital. We had a lovely chat. They are fine people, Charlie, really fine," said Lily. "I thought, there could never be a boy more loved. If you only knew what that means, to be loved. I have no family, none living, that is. I don't know a lot about sailing and fishing or sealing either, but in hospital, I cared for many sailors, Charlie. I saw what the life can do to a man. Maybe," Lily took a breath, "what I mean is, maybe your parents wanted better things for you. Might I be right?"

Charlie drew his knees up to his chin and hugged them tight. He closed his eyes. He could see his father at the head of the table planning out his education with Aunt Maude. There was his mother, happier than he'd ever seen her. Yes, yes, they did want a different life for him. Charlie nodded.

"Maybe then," Lily spoke softly, "coming here was an accident. But staying here, that's different. Maybe you wanted to prove something, not to your parents but to yourself."

"Maybe," Charlie whispered.

"Have you done it yet?" Lily asked.

He shrugged again.

An aeroplane choked and sputtered above them. A Bristol Camel, maybe, on reconnaissance.

Mac took a sip of wine and looked about. "What a strange place we are in. Look at all those tents. One day they will come down, those flimsy buildings will turn to dust, and everything will be as it was. And no one will know of the pain, and death, that happened on this spot. Thing is," Mac took a deep breath, "I don't know if that's a good or bad thing."

"People will remember," said Charlie. "How does that go? 'Those who don't know their history are bound to repeat it' — something like that."

"Why, Charlie, I'm impressed." Lily smiled and Charlie blushed. "But there's another saying. It goes, 'The only thing we learn from history, is that we don't learn from history.'"

"They'll learn," said Charlie confidently and in a near whisper. "There will never be another war like this one. Never."

A thin, warm breeze blew across their faces. Charlie watched as Mac tucked her blonde hair back behind her ears.

Charlie refilled his cup. Yes, very good wine indeed.

"Listen. Hear it?" Mac cocked her head.

"Hear what?" Charlie was looking more than listening. All he could hear was shelling in the distance.

"I thought I heard a bird!"

"I don't hear anything," said Charlie.

"No, I suppose not."

He could see the shape of her head, her nose, her mouth. He moved his hand across the blanket, he reached. His hand hovered over her arm. A current went through him. If he could just . . . if he . . . kiss her? His hand hovered across her back. He leaned forward. Even from here, he could smell her — a delicate smell, the smell of the sea.

"Lily," Charlie whispered.

"Yes, Charlie?" Mac turned her head. Tears stood in her eyes. Her white collar was open. Charlie looked at her long neck and down, until he saw . . . gold. Hanging on a chain around her neck was a gold ring.

"What's that?" his arm snapped back.

Mac looked up, started. Her hand instantly went to her throat. "It's a secret."

"A secret?" Charlie was shaken.

"Charlie, you look offended. I'm sorry. I should tell you. Funny, to find that my best friend is a thirteen-year-old boy!"

"Fourteen," said Charlie, miffed.

"Right, I'm sorry. Here goes." Mac drew a deep breath. "Robert and I are married. There, I've said it. We got married in London three months ago. I keep breaking the rules, don't I? You can't tell anyone, not a soul." Mac made a fist over the ring and closed her eyes. "And there's more. Charlie, I'm to have a baby. Charlie? Charlie, what's the matter?"

The world spun. Jeeze, it did bloody loops! Charlie leaped up, made for a not-too-far lump of earth, and lost his picnic supper.

Mac laughed. "Oh Charlie, darling, are you all right? I guess you're not as old as you thought. Look, you've near taken in the whole bottle."

Charlie sat on his haunches and looked up. The aeroplane dipped out from under broken clouds.

He staggered back and collapsed beside Mac. A baby. What was he supposed to say? What was there to say? In Brigus women used to say that a baby was a blessing, a gift.

"I hear tell," said Charlie slowly, as he watched the aeroplane dip and swoop, "that babies bring good luck."

"Oh, Charlie." Mac threw her arms around him, "Thank you. You said exactly the right thing."

Chapter 18

"*I*t's tomorrow," Mac folded a bedsheet and stacked it on the trolley. "The Great Push."

Charlie handed Mac another bedsheet and nodded. Everyone knew it. Heck, even the Huns knew it. They sat in their own trenches across no-man's-land and held up signs saying just that! Cheeky beggars.

"Your father's letter said that you had to be in England by July 2," said Mac. "That's in two days. Charlie, you should leave today — you should have left yesterday! Think on it, in two or three weeks you'll be home."

"It only takes three hours to cross the Channel," said Charlie as he wandered over to the opening in the tent. The rain had backed off, tomorrow would be grand. A grand day to kill or get killed.

Mac came up behind Charlie and looked out, too. "If it weren't for the guns . . ." No need to say more. It was always the guns, a distant rumble like a thunder.

Mac patted her tummy without thinking. The baby wasn't showing, but it wouldn't be long now. A victory would likely bring Dr. Daniels back from the field hospital. He'd been out in the field since he arrived in France, it's where he wanted to be. She had thought him brave, but now? Now she wanted him safe. Mac had a letter from him a few days back, smuggled in by a wounded soldier. He loved her, he had said that over and over. He couldn't tell her exactly where he was but, between the hints in the letter, and information pried from the wounded soldier, Mac was sure he was one hundred miles away in Auchonvillers or Louvencourt, a stone's throw from the battle that would take place in front of Beaumont Hamel. He would be in the thick of the Great Push, and he had no way of knowing that Mac was going to have their baby.

Charlie looked back at the rows of wounded soldiers. "Why do I get to go home when they have to stay? Just because they are a few years older?" Charlie turned and faced Mac. "Mac, are you all right?" Mac tottered on her heels. Charlie caught her as she stumbled. "Come, sit." Charlie walked her to a chair. Mac slumped over and put her head in her hands.

"Can anyone see?" Mac whispered.

Charlie looked around. Only a soldier, himself too weak to sit up, watched the two.

"No, no one," Charlie winked at the soldier who winked back. "You're not well. It's you who has to go home, Mac."

"No, not yet." Mac lifted her head. The room swayed and she hung her head down again.

"Charlie, I think I'm going to be sick!"

"Here." Charlie grabbed a sick tray and shoved it under her chin. He was good at this. He was good at a lot of things now.

"Thank you. Oh, I feel terrible. How come they call it 'morning sickness' when it lasts all day?" Mac smiled, at least she tried to.

"Who's going to help you when I'm gone?" Charlie put the tray alongside others and passed Mac a cloth.

"This will pass," she said, in such a small voice Charlie had to bend close to hear.

Whenever he could, Charlie covered for her. If she was to move a patient, Charlie was right beside her and did the shifting himself. The other nurses might have noticed had they not been so overworked themselves.

Mac brushed a strand of blonde hair from her face and gave a half-hearted smile.

"I wish I could get a message to him, Charlie. Somehow, just to tell him. What if something happened, what if he never knew?"

"If he did know, he'd say, 'go home.' You know he would."

"I can't. I can't leave him."

"Mac," Charlie took a breath. "Maybe Dr. Daniels will be fine, maybe he won't. You can't protect him. But you can protect your baby." It wasn't the best argument in the world, but it was the best he could do.

Mac might have cried on the spot had Sister not come down the ward, stopped dead in the middle, and clapped her hands. "Sisters, a staff meeting immediately."

"Mac, leave. I'll make up something," Charlie whispered.

Mac clutched the back of the chair and stood. "I'm fine. Really, fine." Setting her veil right and smoothing her apron down with both hands, Mac squared her shoulders and walked past the rows of patients.

A meeting of the medical staff always preceded a major battle. That went hand in hand with a major clean-up. Wounded (those who could be moved) had left for England that very morning. Supplies were checked. Bandages wrapped and stocked in appropriate places. Floors swept. They were ready.

They were never ready.

It would be a few hours after the battle began before they would see their first casualties. They could near set their watches to it. If the battle began at 7:00 in the morning, the first casualties would appear in their wards around noon.

The wounded had their own gauntlet to go through before they could lay down their heads on a proper hospital pillow. Those wounded soldiers who made it back to the trench would be treated by the RAP (Regimental Aid Post) where they were given the most basic of basic care. Then it was off to an ADS (Advance Dressing Station). Here the wounded would be sorted out — who would die, who needed stabilizing, who could be patched up and sent back. The walking wounded got the attention first. If they could walk, hobble even, they were patched up and sent back to the front. Next stop was the FDS (Field Dressing Station). Here dressings were changed, bleeding stopped, broken limbs splintered, shrapnel removed from wounds. All this was done without anesthetic, under dim, swinging lights sometimes in tents or sometimes in the basements of old farmhouses.

Then it was on to the CCS (Casualty Clearing Station), a small hospital where emergency amputations were done, casts were put on, and the wounded languished until they could be moved again. Those soldiers who had the look of death on them were made as comfortable as possible, and left to lie, and die, in the fields.

Dr. Robert Daniels was in an ADS, a field hospital, but he had often been found in a clearing station — and right in the trenches, too.

"JUST TAKE SIPS." Charlie was holding a cup to a soldier's lips when Mac came flying back into the tent.

"It's big, Charlie, but they are talking victory. Victory, Charlie! They say that this is the battle that will turn it all around." Mac wobbled on her feet and gripped the back of a chair. Small beads of sweat glued wisps of hair to her forehead.

"Mac, you have got to tell them. You have to go home." Charlie folded the blankets up around the soldier and stood beside Mac. He would have put his arm around her if he could.

"No, not yet." Mac sat down on the chair and wiped her forehead.

Charlie sighed. "If you could get a message to Dr. Daniels, what would you say?"

Mac hardly stopped to think. "That I love him. That he's to be a father. That he has to stay alive. It's a girl, Charlie,

I just know it. I want a girl. I never want to see a son of mine go to war, never." Mac put her hands to her face as if they would stop the tears. It didn't work.

"Charlie," a voice of authority bellowed behind him.

Charlie spun on his heels and blocked Sister Ruth from seeing Mac. "Yes, ma'am."

"Take this box of supplies over to the ambulance. It's going to Auchonvillers," said Sister Ruth, turning to go.

"Yes, ma'am. Wait," Charlie ran after her. "Auchonvillers, isn't that near Beaumont Hamel?"

"I believe it is," she replied. "The supply will go to Auchonvillers by ambulance and then onto the Beaumont Hamel field hospital."

That's it! Dr. Daniels was at Beaumont Hamel. Mac could get a letter through! Charlie spun around. Where'd she go?

"Charlie, put that in the ambulance!" repeated Sister Ruth. "What is wrong with you?"

"Nothing."

"Then hurry." Sister Ruth hustled ahead of him.

Charlie took a last look for Mac.

"Charlie!" Sister Ruth hollered.

"Coming." Charlie ran behind Sister Ruth to the waiting ambulance and tossed the boxes into the back.

"There are a few more boxes. Come on," said Sister Ruth.

"Right behind you." Charlie took the steps two by two. Sister Ruth took a right; Charlie took a left. Within moments he was back in his sleeping quarters, or rather his broom closet. He took out a pen and paper, and began to scribble.

Dear Mac,

I am going to find Dr. Daniels and I will tell him your news. I have to leave because if I stay you will not take my ticket home. If you don't take the ticket, it will be a waste. Once you tell Matron-in-Chief, she'll send you packing fast anyway, but we both know that it may be months before you get a berth. And I think that if you don't go home very soon, you will get sick and lose your baby.

I've enclosed the letter from my father. It tells you what to do. My parents will take care of you. Tell my parents and sisters that I love them. But don't tell them too much else.

See you in Newfoundland,
Charlie.

Charlie jammed his letter, and the letter from his father, into an envelope. He pulled his sealer's boots out from under his cot and yanked them on. The chisels and sparables, hobnails really, made clinks against the wood floor. He'd need his oil-slick sweater. What else? It was hard to think. Charlie grabbed his haversack, shoved in the sweater, and just as he turned to leave, spotted the spy glass. It had come this far, he wouldn't leave it now. He stuck it in the pack, slung it over his back, and raced back down the steps.

"Where did you go?" Sister Ruth wasn't pleased but she was too busy to be furious. She dumped another box into Charlie's arms.

"Sorry. Can you give this to Mac? It's important." Sister Ruth took the letter.

"Yes. Tell the driver that this is the last load. Go."

"Don't forget," Charlie yelled after her.

"I won't. Go." Sister Ruth flew back into a tent and Charlie loaded the boxes into the back of the ambulance.

"That's it then, boy." The driver grinned as he shut and secured the first of two doors on the lorry. Charlie looked again. The driver wasn't a he, he was a she! Shod in gum boots, and wearing a mackintosh that near dusted the ground, it was hard to tell. The driver, a FANY, grabbed hold of the second door.

"Right. Let me do that." Charlie grabbed hold of the second door.

"Good lad. Beastly business, isn't it?" The driver didn't wait for a reply but hopped into the front seat of the lorry, just as Charlie scrambled into the back. He slammed the door after him. Auchonvillers was one hundred miles away — a couple of hours maybe. Nevertheless, it took the better part of the day to get there. Mind, it might have been faster had the driver not tried to hit every pothole in France. Boxes, labeled "fragile," took turns falling on his head.

The sound of the guns grew with each passing mile.

They reached Auchonvillers by dusk. The lorry came to an abrupt stop; the boxes did not. Jeeze.

Charlie opened the door of the lorry a crack and peeked out. The driver jumped out and made for the Salvation Army canteen, which was nothing more than a tin hut with a window hacked out in the side. Charlie leaped down, put on his pack, adjusted his Red Cross armband, and made like he was taking a summer's day stroll. Beaumont Hamel would be just up the road. He just had to figure out which road.

Small bands of men drilled up and down; others sat smoking and polishing their Lee Enfields. In the distance Charlie could see some men kicking around a football. Another group seemed to be cleaning out a tent. It was all rather civilized. Except for the distant shelling, it could be peacetime anywhere with just a bunch of lads mucking about.

"Ah, sir," Charlie called out to a soldier. The soldier's cap and the collar of his tunic bore a caribou badge — he was from the Newfoundland Regiment. "I'm to report to the nearest Field Dressing Station." Charlie spoke bravely.

"What? Is the Red Cross recruiting school boys now?" The soldier laughed.

"I'm thirty-six years old, sir. Where is the FDS?"

"Smart-aleck." The soldier grinned. "There's an old farm house down the road. That's it." He turned to leave.

"Ah, sir," Charlie ran after him. "Do you know where the Newfoundlanders of the 29th Division is? I have friends in it."

"In the trenches in front of Beaumont Hamel."

"That's where I want to go — Beaumont Hamel."

"Then you be sure to give Fritz our best."

Charlie, more confused than ever, sputtered, "Hu?"

"Beaumont Hamel is in enemy hands, boy. But tell you what. You want to pop on by, go ahead. Bring back a beer. Heard good things about German beer." The soldier turned to walk away. Charlie scampered alongside.

"Wait. I'm looking for the Newfoundlanders." Jeeze, it was a simple enough question.

"The Newfoundlanders haven't arrived yet. They're on

the march. Arriving anytime I expect. But you'll find the rest of the 29th Division on St. John's Road."

"St. John's Road?"

"A forward trench, boy." The soldier stopped and glared down at Charlie. The Great Push was on and giving a lesson to some ignorant boy was not in the plans. "All the trenches are called after street names from home."

Charlie looked as confused as ever.

"See here," the soldier pushed up his cap until it sat on the back of his head. "There are dozens of connecting trenches but three main ones. The one closest to the front is called the fire trench. The one behind it is the support trench. The third one is the reserve trench. The trench that connects them all is the communication trench. The 29th are in the trenches directly in front of Beaumont Hamel. Do ya follow me, boy, or are you thick?"

A blast drowned out anything more that might have been said. Charlie ducked; the soldier meandered away.

"You there, medic," yelled a lorry driver. Charlie had never seen him before.

Charlie looked about. "Me?"

"Bloody right, you," snapped back the driver. "Get in."

This time Charlie sat in the front seat of the lorry. Off they went. The roads were thick with transport — wagons carrying ammunitions and rations, some hauling hay for horses, barrels of water and food, too. There were motorbikes and ambulances, troops going every which way, and long lines of mules and horses that left droppings big enough to be climbed over. Fancy automobiles passed, too, the likes of which Charlie hadn't seen before.

"Officers," scowled the driver as he nodded in the direction of an automobile as big as a small boat. A Daimler they called it.

Coming toward them, and against all the traffic, were ragtag locals pushing carts or hauling huge bundles on their backs or heads. An exhausted family of ten or more trudged passed so close to the truck that Charlie could see the tops of their heads and individual strands of hair. They had a look in their eyes — not of defeat, but something worse than that. Coping had replaced hoping.

Soldiers with red armbands and red hats stood watching from the sides: military police on the lookout for spies. Occasionally, one pulled over a local person and asked questions, checked papers. They had another job, too. They were watching for deserters, and if they found one, he was captured, tried in a military court, and then shot.

Dust came toward them like giant rolling tumbleweeds. And just when the shelling could get no louder, it got louder.

"Where are we going?" Charlie hollered.

"The front."

"How far . . ." Three blasts, one after the other, drowned out Charlie. "How far is the front?" He screamed this time.

"Not far enough." The lorry hit a pothole. Charlie nearly went through the roof. "They need replacement stretcher-bearers."

"I'm not a stretcher-bearer."

"You are now."

Chapter 19

Charlie hung onto the overhead strap for dear life. "Where'd you learn to drive?" he hollered.

"Hu?"

"Drive? Where did you learn?"

"Learn? No, I never learned to drive."

The lorry bumped along the muddy road, hit the ditch a few times, swerved back to fall into the watery ruts, and then came to an abrupt stop at a town called Mailly Maillet.

"Front lines," the driver pointed to a hill, "over there."

Charlie scrambled out of the lorry and looked up to a light show. Like demented fireflies, the shells flew up into the evening sky to create a sudden, brilliant light. In a hairpin turn, they took swan dives into the ground and for a moment, it was as if the earth was set on fire.

Charlie and the driver stumbled across a field and clambered over the hill until they saw a sign. It read Tipperary Avenue.

They could smell the trenches before they could see them. The stench rose up in great waves. The entire area reeked of shell fire, gasoline, urine, feces, unwashed bodies, and all things rotting and wrong.

"Down there," hollered the driver, "you'll see the aid post." The driver turned back as Charlie stumbled down the mud-steps into a maze of trenches.

"Where's the 29th?" Charlie yelled at a soldier who stood not two feet away.

"Keep going."

Charlie put his hand against the mud wall to steady himself. Sure enough, at the beginning of the trench a sign read, "St. John's Road." Beside it was an aid post. A small man, himself a stretcher-bearer with a Red Cross band on his arm, crouched low under a shield of tin.

"You the replacement?" he hollered.

Charlie nodded.

"Where's your uniform? And where's your helmet?" he asked, and not kindly.

Charlie shrugged and ducked at the same time. A shell landed nearby and dirt kicked up over him.

"Well, that near took the head off ya. No need for a helmet then, hey?" The stretcher-bearer laughed heartily and tossed him a helmet. It had a red cross painted on the front and, in one side, a bullet hole. Charlie stuck his finger through it. A skull must have stopped the bullet from coming out the other side.

"It goes on your head," yelled the stretcher-bearer.

"They like to pick us off because we're moving targets."

"But they're not supposed to shoot the Red Cross." Charlie hollered back as loud as he could.

"Maybe Fritz can't tell us from the runners. But then, maybe they can!" The stretcher-bearer yelled over the blasts. Three shells dropped, one after another.

"What's a runner?" yelled Charlie.

"You new?"

Jeeze, Charlie knew better than to ask questions.

"Communications. Messengers. Carry information. They last maybe twenty-four, forty-eight hours before they're picked off by a sniper."

"Stretcher-bearer!" A shout came from down the line.

The stretcher-bearer jumped and grabbed one end of the litter.

"Keep your head down," he yelled over his shoulder.

Charlie took hold of the back end of the litter and ran. He may have been running with it, or being dragged by it. He couldn't tell.

The trenches were narrow and dark. Sandbags, piled like bricks, lined the top. Duckboards, strips of wood, were underfoot, but it was near impossible to get his footing right. The wood sagged in places and, in others, disappeared all together. Charlie's feet splashed into a muddy hole. Next, he was on higher ground, then down again. On either side, soldiers gave way. Some of them, even with the roar of war going on around them, slept. Others kept to their posts, grim faces, blackened by shell fire and mud. They looked like coal miners.

The trench zigzagged this way and that. It was made that way so if a bomb dropped in, it wouldn't blast straight down the lines. And if Fritz jumped in with a machine gun, he couldn't kill off the whole platoon in one spurt of fire. But it made it damn difficult to get the litter through.

The first of the wounded they picked up that night was young. Maybe nineteen years old. His tunic, soaked through with blood, had turned purple. It was the only thing holding him together.

"Mother," cried the boy, "Mother."

"Run, kid, run," yelled the stretcher-bearer. This time Charlie gave no thought to his head bouncing up over the top of the trench. He just ran.

Back at the aid post, two orderlies took the wounded boy away.

"I hates it when they does that," said the stretcher-bearer, who plunked himself down on a crate and fished around his tunic for his cigarettes.

"Does what?"

"Calls out for their mother. Means they are going to die."

Charlie slumped down, his back pressed up against the mud wall of the trench. "Is it always like this?"

"Heck, no. This is great. Just you wait for tomorrow. Then you'll see some real action." The stretcher-bearer lit a cig and let it dangle from his mouth. He reached into a pack that hung around his belly and pulled out a tin. With a twist of a wrist he opened a can of bully beef. A hunk of stewed meat went in his mouth alongside the cigarette. A thin line of juice trickled down his chin.

"Ruffff." A little dog let out a high-pitched bark. Charlie near jumped out of his skin.

"What's a dog doing here?" asked Charlie.

"Ah?"

"I said, what's a dog doing here?" Charlie yelled this time.

"It's on a mission," yelled back the stretcher-bearer between bites and puffs. "Taking communications back and forth, maybe."

"Where did it come from?" Charlie yelled again.

"Fire trench, I expect," said the stretcher-bearer.

"No, I mean before that."

"Oh, families in England mostly. They give up the family pets for the war effort," hollered the medic. "That mutt was probably sitting on a pink satin pillow six months ago, and eating chopped liver, maybe. Them dogs that can be trained turns into good little runners. It's the Brits that has them. This one must'a lost its way."

After the dog came a fat, furry rat. The medic swiped at it with his boot, but it paid him no mind and carried on down the line.

"Ya know, the first time I saw one of those rats, I thought they was some sort of ugly, fat French cat." The medic laughed and took a long drag. "Get some sleep, if ya can."

"Can't. I need to get to the field dressing station. I have a message for Dr. Robert Daniels," said Charlie.

"Best wait for first light then. Here, eat something." The medic tossed Charlie what was left of the tin of bully beef. Two small hunks of shredded meat swam around in a pool of oil.

"Thanks." Charlie knocked it back fast — less taste that way. He would have chucked the tin aside had the medic not grabbed it back.

"Streets paved of tin," chuckled the stretcher-bearer as he hammered the tin into the ground and stamped on it. Right enough, now that Charlie looked closely, where the duckboards ended, hundreds of tins lined the floor of the trench.

Charlie opened his pack and pulled on his oil-slick sweater, the same one his mother made him. It was June 30, summer by all accounts, but cold anyway. He crawled into a shelf, a funk hole they called it, that had been carved into the trench wall. Charlie put his haversack under his head, pulled his feet in after him, and curled up as best he could.

IT WAS A DREAM he was in. All he had to do was wake up and he'd be in his own bed. He could almost feel his pillowcase under his head, the one with the little red and blue flowers embroidered around the edges. The walls were papered with yellow flowers dangling from green stems, blooming summer and winter. His feet would be warm from the heated stones his mother had slipped into the bottom of his bed. Emma would be hollering at him for something or other, and his mother would have warm bread on the table, cut extra thick with two servings of molasses on top. Everything — the trenches, the bombs, the rats — was a dream. It had to be. Parents wouldn't send their children to die like this.

Chapter 20

Sleep was impossible. The shelling was relentless. Charlie dozed in his coffin-shaped funk hole, but snapped to when he heard the thuds of stomping feet. In through the trench poured a steady stream of men. It was the Newfoundlanders, all right. Some looking pensive, some champing at the bit. Months of waiting, lining up for food, showers, mail, months of drills and training all came down to this battle — a battle that would turn the tides and send them all home. God was with them, and the love of thems at home too.

From his funk hole, Charlie watched the blur of brown uniforms pass, and then they were gone. He looked around for the stretcher-bearer. He was gone, too. Charlie never even knew his name.

Hungry, Charlie swung his haversack onto his back and started down the trenches. Which way was the way out? The shelling continued, raining down on either side. First there was a shrill whistle as a shell whizzed through the air, and then a thump and a boom as it hit. Occasionally a machine gun would spit out a *rat-a-tat-tat*, like a furious woodpecker. One big blast lit up the sky, and for a moment it was day.

He needed a latrine.

"Where's the loo?" Charlie shouted into a soldier's ear. Begrudgingly, and half asleep, the man pointed to the front.

"Out there."

Charlie couldn't take it in.

"No, where is the latrine?" He yelled louder this time.

"It's in a dugout out there. They put 'em toward the front so no man dallies. Tell ya right," the soldier sneered, "you'll not be wanting to hang about in a loo, not with Fritz takin' aim at your butt."

Charlie, like most, did his business against the mud wall of the trench.

Carrying on, he stumbled over legs and packs. Some soldiers stared ahead, blurry-eyed and lost; others were wild with excitement. Most just sat, warming their hands around tea in tin cups and chewing biscuits.

Suddenly a hand reached out and Charlie was pinned to the mud wall.

"Why the hell are you here? I told you to go home." Martin, his lips pulled thin and the muscles on his neck standing out, had Charlie by the throat. "You were to get on the next ship home. You're an idiot, no smarter than a seal waiting for a whack."

The spit in Charlie's throat near choked him. "Martin, I . . ."

"Let him go, Martin." Michael gave Martin a shove. He let go and Charlie slid down the wall to land on his behind.

Michael and Martin stared down at Charlie. Martin spoke first.

"Ah, Charlie, I didn't mean to hurt you. I'm going balmy." Martin looked tired and worn. "Come here, boy." He reached down and helped Charlie to his feet. "You all right?"

Charlie put his hand to his neck and nodded.

"Well, it's the adventure of a lifetime, isn't it?" Martin laughed. He took off his tin hat and rubbed his forehead with the back of his sleeve.

"It's good to see you, boy," said Michael, as he rolled a cigarette, one that contained as much mud as tobacco. He lit it and passed it to Charlie. Charlie, not a smoker, took a drag anyway. Martin passed Charlie a biscuit and his own mug of tea, and for a while no one spoke.

The commander, a small, dapper fellow with a sad look, came down the line, talking to soldiers as he went. He squeezed past Charlie, not giving him so much as a glance.

Michael and Martin struggled to their feet and gave a sorry attempt at a salute.

"At ease, boys. It looks like a civil day ahead." He had a kind face, the face of a school teacher maybe. "Just think, this time tomorrow the tide will be turned. Poor bloody beggars. We've got hundreds of battalions and enough ammo to blow up France. Fritz won't know what hit 'em. Got your identification triangle stitched on?" Michael and Martin nodded. Each soldier was issued tin triangles that were to be sewn onto their backs. They would make identification easy from behind, or from an aeroplane.

The commander made a cursory inspection of their Lee Enfields and asked about ammo. "We'll have 'em all on the run, I tell you. Have you your assigned load?" He was referring to the extra weight, on top of the usual sixty pounds, that each man had to carry over the top, the parapet they called it.

"Yes, sir," said Michael sharply, and with respect.

Soldiers were expected to carry sandbags, sledge hammers, shovels — anything and everything they would need to make the enemy trenches livable and civilized. How could they have known that the German trenches were deep, that their bunkers went down thirty or more feet, that some officers' quarters were lined with wallpaper? That in one trench, they would discover a baby grand piano.

Martin and Michael were to haul the trench ladder. It would be used as a bridge over the trenches in front of them. That, plus the regulation sixty pounds, would make running a challenge. No matter. This charge was a cakewalk. Everyone said so. What with the bombing and such. In fact, it wasn't a charge at all. More like a stroll across no-man's-land and breezy saunter into Fritz's camp. Charlie said nothing, just watched it all like it was a play.

"Just do what's right, with all your might boys." The commander said as he moved on down the trench. His uniform matched the mud walls so well it was if he disappeared all together.

"That's what me mother used to say," Michael piped up. The shelling on either side was stepping up. "*Sleep tight, to wake up bright in the morning light, to do what's right with all your might."*

"Bet she didn't say nothin' about shootin' Fritz's head off," said Martin with a half-hearted grin. "Right, boy?" He looked at Charlie, who, numbed with the noise, only nodded back.

"You got one there, Martin-boy?" Michael looked Martin's way.

Martin shook his head. He didn't particularly want to recall a time when he was a boy and his mother tucked him, and his brother, into the great brass bed. If he closed his eyes he could almost smell the woolly blankets that were dried out in the salty air.

"Angels above, angels below, keep me safe wherever I go," Martin whispered.

Then came a wash of bombardment, so loud, so long, no voice could reach above it. The sheer sound forced every soldier to crouch down and cover his head.

"Down, Charlie," Martin hollered. Grabbing Charlie by the scruff of his neck, he pushed him down and covered him as best he could. Charlie was near smothered by the weight of Martin. Then came two more blasts, strong and deafening. The very ground they crouched on shivered. Tons of earth was flung up into the air, and for a second it hung there, suspended, before it poured down like rain. Later they'd say the bombs were heard across the Channel in London.

A SOLDIER CAME DOWN the lines with a draft of rum. He poured it into the waiting cups of the soldiers. Martin heaved it down in one gulp. Michael refused. It was a promise he made to his mother, never to touch spirits.

"Not long now, boys. We'll do our bit, make 'em all proud," said the fellow with the rum.

Martin turned to Charlie and whispered right into his ear, his voice crackling with worry. "Listen here, boy, you're not to move from this spot. You get me, Charlie? You hear me, boy? You coopy down until this is all over. You're not to move, no matter what happens. Promise?"

Charlie nodded.

"Say it."

"I promise."

"As a Newfoundlander."

"As a Newfoundlander."

"Good. Good." Once again, Martin took his position.

It was Michael who started it. With his head bowed he said, "*The Lord is my shepherd; I shall not want. He maketh me to lie down in green pastures; He leadth me beside the still waters; He restoreth my soul.*"

Jeeze, they couldn't hear a shout, but they heard this. One by one, men down the line joined in. The words were whispered, heard not by the ears, but by the heart.

"*He leadth me in the path of righteousness for his name's sake. Yea, though I walk through the valley of the shadow of death, I will fear no evil; for thou art with me. Thy rod and thy staff they comfort me. Thou preparest a table before me in the presence of mine enemies; Thou anointest my head with oil; My cup runneth over.*"

And to the sky Michael called out, "*Surely goodness and mercy shall follow me all the days of my life: And I shall dwell in the house of the Lord forever.*"

And up and down the line, "*Amen.*"

Michael stood still for a moment. He turned and then passed a piece of paper to Charlie. "I want you to take this. It's to my mother." Michael dropped the smudged letter into Charlie's lap. "Go on, Charlie, take it."

"Stand-to." The order came down the ranks. With bayonets clamped to the muzzles of their guns, Martin and Michael took their positions on the fire steps. The trench ladder was propped up against the mud wall beside them.

The Brits had already gone over the top. By now they would be through their own barbed wire, which lay like a small girl's ringlets across no-man's-land. Past what would one day be called the Danger Tree — a beleaguered, bald, and dead collection of sticks that hung by its roots over a shell hole. It refused, or had forgotten, to fall down. It was the only marking left in an otherwise barren landscape. The Brits, the Irish, and the Newfoundlanders would use it to get their bearings. There they would collect, and there the Germans would mow them down.

A short distance from that was the enemy's own curly barbed wire. No fear, there were plenty of holes in that wire to crawl through — that's what they were told. It wasn't true.

But, boy, it was soupy out there. A morning fog, combined with the shelling, had turned a bright summer's day into twilight. You could hardly see your nose.

"What do ya think God thinks about all this?" whispered Michael.

The whistle blew.

The men yelled a charge. Blood pumped, breath short, the first wave leaped up and over the sandbags like they were being pulled forward by some mystical rope. This was it, victory was at hand!

Michael and Martin were soon to follow. Michael took hold of the front of the ladder. Martin, his hands holding the back end, yelled, "Listen to me, Charlie. You go home and tell my father that I did what I was supposed to do. That I didn't let him down. You tell him that."

"I will, Martin. I will." Tears zigzagged down Charlie's face.

Martin reached for Charlie's hand. "Best thing I ever did was get you out of that crate. You're a brave, strong lad, Charlie-boy. God bless."

"And you," Charlie whispered, "and you."

The second wave of Newfoundlanders made themselves ready. Again, the whistle blew.

"That's it, men, over the top." A cheer went up. Martin and Michael heaved the ladder up over the sandbags.

"Come on, boys, we'll have a real cook-up on the other side," said a voice from down the line.

The Newfoundland Regiment clambered out of the rat-infested trench and, toting more weight than a man could carry, staggered into no-man's-land.

"May God take you home, Charlie," yelled Michael over his shoulder. He turned and ran into a hail of greedy bullets.

Chapter 21

$\mathscr{C}$harlie cowered down into the trench and rocked on his haunches. This wasn't real. It couldn't be real. There was another sound besides machine gun fire, and shelling, and the *rat-a-ta-tat* of the machine guns. Men screaming. They screamed for God, for their mothers, for death. Charlie closed his eyes and cupped his hands over his ears to block out the sound. This made it worse, like being in a water barrel with a hailstorm thumping on the outside.

It went on forever, and only for a moment. And then the shelling decreased. Later, when all was tolled, sixty thousand men lay dead within a sixteen-mile stretch of land. They would say that the men fought bravely and well.

A soldier lay at Charlie's feet. He checked his pulse. Nothing. He pushed the body to one side and stepped up to the fire steps. Smoke, that's all there was, and sniper fire. Ping, ping. Charlie crouched down low again. He promised Martin that he'd wait, that he'd stay put. He sat back down on his haunches. He stood up. He sat down. He stood up.

He had had enough. With his haversack on his back, he heaved himself up over the sandbags. Charlie crawled out of the St. John's reserve trench and picked his way across the trench ladder that lay over the fire trench. The trench was a shallow grave of strewn bodies. He lowered himself down amongst them carefully. Here Charlie took the spy glass out of his haversack and brought it to his eye. With the precision of a young sailor, he scanned a sea of smoke. "See," whispered a far-off voice, "not look."

"Father?" Charlie's head jerked up. "Father?"

"See," said the voice again, "see with your heart and your soul, Charlie. Focus."

The smoke opened up in patches. A shell hit. The dirt flew up into the air and dust fell down. Charlie got a fix on the area. "See," Charlie whispered to himself. Nothing. Nothing. Nothing. Another patch opened up and Charlie focused on a face. It was a young face, maybe eighteen years old, and pained, but he was standing. His face was caked in mud. His eyes opened wide in horror, a scared kid, could be any kid. Charlie blinked and refocused. He was looking into the face of the murderous Hun.

Again Charlie swept the battleground. There! Martin was lying face up. Charlie could just make out his profile. His helmet had fallen off, and his white hair shone like a beacon. It was him, sure as anything, and he was moving. He was maybe one hundred yards away. Miles away.

Charlie shoved the spy glass back in the haversack and

dropped it at his feet. No sense carrying extra weight. It landed between the arms and legs of dead and wounded soldiers below.

Charlie crawled out of the fire trench on his belly and headed out toward the barbed wire. A shell landed not five feet from him. He rolled, snake-like, into the smoking crater and waited. Clear. Up and out he scrambled.

"Martin," Charlie whispered, as he inched himself along in the mud, "hang on, I'm coming."

A battle was not something to be seen, it was to be heard. Hear it first, smell it second, and then see it — maybe not at all. Charlie cocked his head and listened. Straining, straining to hear a voice amidst the bombing, the shelling, the shooting, and the screaming. It was near impossible.

"Martin. Martin," Charlie called.

His best cover was the smoke, but that couldn't be depended on. Charlie crawled, wiggled, and squirmed. He wasn't on earth anymore. This was the moon — all rocks, gully, and holes. And the soldiers that littered the moonscape weren't soldiers anymore, just grotesque, alien creatures that lay about on a sea of dust. The dirt in his mouth tasted like gun powder. Mud collected in his nose, ears, and eyes. His hand went down on something sharp. He pulled it back fast and looked at it. No blood. It didn't pierce the skin. He'd seen more than his share of men whose only injury was a simple cut. Mud, infested with every kind of germ, bore into open cuts and wounds, infected and killed as sure as any bullet. Charlie pulled his sleeves down over his hands and used his arms to pull himself along. Once or twice he stuck his butt in the air and ran like an ape. Again and again, he tumbled into a crater only to come up the other side and crawl some more. The shelling had all but ceased. The snipers were having a field day now, picking off anything that moved. Charlie slowed down.

"Martin, Martin," called Charlie.

"Charlie?" Martin called back. "Charlie?" Like he couldn't believe it.

Charlie rolled up to Martin and lay beside him.

"I'm here. It's me." Charlie whispered, mostly sobbed.

"My legs. Jeeze, they're gone." It was a stupor he was in, half-conscious.

"No, they're not. Never mind your legs. Just hold on." Charlie looked down. Martin's leg was near split from the top of his thigh down past his knee. Charlie jammed Martin's helmet back on his head — best to cover up that white hair. He yanked Martin's field dressing kit out of his tunic and ripped open the iodine packet with his teeth. "This is going to hurt, Martin. Real bad." He poured the red liquid into Martin's open wound.

"No, no more. No more. Mother. Mother," Martin screamed and clawed at the air.

"Martin, Martin." Charlie tried to pin Martin's flaying arms down. "Your mother's not here, Martin. There's just me. Get your hands down. Ya have got to stay still, Martin. Don't draw any attention to us. Listen to me, Martin," Charlie cupped his hands around Martin's face and sobbed, his tears mixing with the sweat and mud on Martin's face. "Listen. Legs don't count, I tell you. One of my best friends has no legs and he's going to be a famous artist one day. Legs is just legs. They're not brains. They're not you. Stay with me. I'll get ya help. I will, Martin. You're not going to die on this day, Martin, not this day. Where's your water bottle? You need water. Please God," cried Charlie, as he scrambled about in the mud searching for Martin's own haversack, "please God, don't take him. He's got to go home and get married. He promised. Please, let him live."

Charlie's hand came down on Martin's water bottle. He fumbled with the cap. His hands shook so bad the liquid splashed on the ground.

"It's OK. It's OK," he said, as much to himself as Martin. Slowly Charlie dripped water into Martin's gaping mouth. Bandages, he needed bandages. The field dressing kit had spilled on the ground. He rummaged around. There. He found a length of dressing and made a tourniquet around Martin's leg, all the while keeping his head down.

He did the best he could.

There was nothing to do but wait for nightfall, hours and hours away. Then, Charlie reasoned, they could crawl back to their trench under the cover of night. He curled up beside him and flung an arm over Martin's chest, like he could protect him somehow. All around them the slaughter continued.

THEY LAY, SIDE BY SIDE, for the better part of the day. Martin was now going in and out of consciousness. Once in a while he cried out, words Charlie didn't understand.

"It's OK, you're going to be OK," Charlie repeated, over and over. He lifted Martin's eyelids. His eyes, sunk back into his head, were glazing over.

"You need to drink more water, Martin," and again

Charlie dribbled water into Martin's mouth. It did no good. He just coughed it up. Martin would die if they stayed there much longer. He had to do something. Charlie bound Martin's wound as tightly as he dared. Snake-like, wiggling, he rolled over to another soldier. He was a lieutenant. No pulse. Satisfied he was dead, Charlie yanked off the officer's belt and made his way back to Martin.

"Martin, I'm going to lash you to my back. Don't fight me. Just think of yourself as a great big fish, a whale maybe. Think on that, Martin, fishing. Fishing off the Labrador. I mean to do that, Martin. Maybe we can do it together, ah? I mean to sail with Bob Bartlett himself. You can come to, if you're not busy with that household of kids. Are you listening? We got plans, Martin. Think of . . ." Charlie searched his brain. What was her name? "Meeta. Think of Meeta. We don't have far to go, maybe a hundred feet. We'll make it, we will."

Charlie put the belt under Martin and rolled on top of him. "Right now." The belt ran over one shoulder and under the other arm. He buckled it tightly around his own chest and rolled again. Martin was strapped to Charlie's back.

Charlie began to crawl, inch by inch. It was the boots that saved them. His father's sealer's boots with the sparables and chisels embedded in the soles and heels of the boots helping him to push off. He used his hands to claw and pull himself forward. Slowly, painfully, Charlie clawed his way back across the pitted ground. Sweat poured down his face like the march of army ants, itching and blinding him. He couldn't stop to wipe it away. There was no air to breathe. It was all gun power and stench.

More than once Charlie found shelter behind bodies that had fallen in a heap. Still, single bullets seemed to target them.

"What is it? How can they see us?" Charlie stopped at a bullet-ridden corpse. He, too, was a Newfoundlander. On his back was a shiny plate with the markings of their regiment. The sun, hardly reaching the ground through the smoke, gave off a dim reflection, like a tarnished mirror might.

"You're wearing a bloody target," yelled Charlie, and he rolled over near squishing Martin in the process. Charlie unlashed Martin as fast as he could, rolled him back over, and ripped off the plate. It started to make sense. When the soldiers found that they couldn't break through the barbed wire, they'd turn around and look for another way. But with the targets on their backs all Fritz had to do was aim! Bloody hell.

"We'll be fine now. Martin, you hear me?"

Charlie dragged and pushed Martin. Corpses got in the way, soldiers no more. He shoved them aside and tried not to think of them as men. He tried not to think at all.

Almost there. Then more shots. Charlie fell over Martin. Slowly he lifted his head to look around. There! There! The bullets were coming from their own lines! They were being shot at by their own men!

"Newfoundland, Newfoundland!" Charlie screamed as loud as he could.

Their trench was within sight. "Newfoundland." Charlie crawled up on his knees pulling Martin by the shoulders. "Newfoundland." They both fell backward into the trench.

"Stretcher-bearer!" Charlie tried to catch his breath.

"Stretcher-bearer! Martin, wake up. Martin, it's OK now. The war is over for you. It's time to go home, Martin."

If he kept talking then Martin would stay alive. No one talks to a dead man. Martin was alive, just passed out. Charlie felt for a pulse. Weak, but there. No iodine left. Charlie reached and touched a soldier who was slouched over not four feet away. He felt his wrist, then his neck. No pulse. None. He yanked the soldier's tunic open and pulled out the dead man's field dressing kit. "Martin, you'll not feel this, so I might as well give you another dose.

"Stretcher-bearer!" Charlie kept up the call like a forlorn fog horn. "Stretcher-bearer! OK, Martin, I'm just going to rip your pants and take a look at this leg. Now, I know that you're awfully fond of your uniform, but I'm sure they'll give you a new one — stretcher-bearer! — once you explain that it was me, not you, that ripped it." Charlie tore off the makeshift bandage he had made, gripped both sides of Martin's pant leg, and ripped it wide open.

A startlingly white bone shot through the skin. "Stretcher-bearer! I've seen worse, Martin-boy. Matter of fact, they just might call you a sloucher for taking a nap midway through the battle. It's clean. You'll make it just fine. I'll just fix the tourniquet and you'll be set right." Charlie set to work. "Stretcher-bearer! There now." He reached up and undid Martin's jacket. "This should make you more comfortable. Oh, mother of God, oh . . ."

A hole the size of an orange gaped from Martin's side. Charlie rolled Martin over. There was a bullet's entrance hole, but no exit. The bullet was still in him. "Stretcher-bearer!" Charlie stood and with all that was left in him screamed as loud as he could. "Stretcher-bearer!" He fell, resting his head on Martin's shoulder and he sobbed. "I'm sorry. I'm sorry."

"Move off." Two stretcher-bearers came round the bend. Charlie slumped down onto his haunches as they rolled Martin onto the litter and ran off with him. Dazed, Charlie stumbled a bit, and then scrambled to keep up. He should have checked. He should have checked for other wounds. He knew better. He was stupid, stupid.

Charlie stumbled, tripped, stumbled again, down the line, stepping over one body then another.

"Hey, you, move them out of the way," yelled another stretcher-bearer from behind. "We can't get through." Like he was moving lumber, Charlie shifted bodies to either side of the trench. A blanket lay over the face of one body. Gripping the tunic of the soldier, he heaved, and stopped. Something made this body different from all the rest. Something in the sight of his broad back and large hands. Charlie reached down and pulled away the rough, filthy blanket. It was Michael.

His face was the color of chalk, shrunken and shriveled. Crusts of mud had formed over his cheeks and forehead, and his lips were cracked and caked with dried, black blood.

"Oh, Michael, no."

Charlie fell to his knees and wrapped his arms around him, like Michael's own mother might have. He held him close for a moment. Gently, as if not to wake him, Charlie reached into Michael's tunic and pulled out his Bible. "I'll see that it gets home, Michael. As best I can." Charlie took Michael's field dressing kit and replaced the blanket over his face.

He came up to the aid station. A medic had just finished giving Martin a once-over.

"Where's he going?" asked Charlie in a raspy voice.

"Nowhere," said the medic. "Next."

"What do you mean, next?" It was all Charlie could do to talk. His breath was short.

"He's not going to make it. Put him over there." The medic spied Charlie's dirty Red Cross armband. "Do it and get to work." The medic moved away to examine others.

To the left, men lay on the ground, waiting to die. To the right, men moaned softly or lay in stunned silence, waiting for transport by lorry, or by a small push-train, powered by a mule and men, to take them to the Field Dressing Station.

Charlie lingered. He fidgeted with a bandage, and when the medic was out of earshot he called out, "You, stretcher-bearer, help me move him."

The stretcher-bearer bent down, heaved his end of the litter up, and started to move Martin to the side.

"No," said Charlie. "Over there. To the right."

"That bunch are waiting for transport."

"Yea, he's to be transported out," said Charlie.

"Doesn't look like he'll make it to me."

"Medic's orders." Charlie shrugged and tried not to appear too eager.

The stretcher-bearer shrugged too. Together they rolled Martin onto a rail car of the push-train.

Charlie bent down and whispered in Martin's ear. "Here's the deal. I'll keep you alive if you stay alive, OK, Martin? You have got to fight real hard."

Charlie took the iodine from his pocket and dropped it into Martin's opened wound. "This one's from Michael."

The push-train rolled forward. Martin, Charlie, and a half dozen wounded men were on their way to a FDS. Not ten minutes later the train stopped at a broken-down stone farmhouse. The two-story house was attached to a barn on one side and a smaller building on the other. Together they formed a small courtyard. Scattered around, a hundred or so men lay in the cobbled courtyard or farther out on the damp earth. Some lay in muddy pools waiting to be patched up and sent back to the front, or to die right where they were. The lucky few would see a hospital by day's end. Luckier still would be the soldier who would make it all the way to England.

"Careful." Charlie hovered as two stretcher-bearers lifted Martin off the rail car and placed him on the ground. "Where's the doctor?" Charlie asked. "He needs attention."

"The doctor's in there," the stretcher-bearer pointed to the farmhouse. "Expect he's a bit busy."

Charlie bent down and whispered in Martin's ear, "We're at the field hospital, Martin. It won't be long now." Charlie folded Martin's arms across his chest, took off his own sweater, and wrapped it around Martin. "Stay put, ya hear me? Don't go wandering off. I'm just going to have a little talk with the doctor."

Charlie walked toward the farmhouse. He stepped carefully between, and over, bodies of men, some passed out, a few dead.

The door to the farmhouse had long since fallen off. He walked down a dim hall, dodging hunks of plaster that hung from the ceiling by threads. To the right was a parlor with worn velvet chairs, a gold-ribbed settee, scattered tables piled high with dirty mugs — there were even books on the shelves. He came to where the kitchen must have once been, when it was a home. A medic passed by carrying a basin of crimson water and stained towels.

"Where is the doctor?" Charlie asked.

"Operating," was all he said.

Charlie walked through the kitchen and out a door and found himself in the backyard. What he saw near took his breath away. In the distance, graves were being dug, mass graves. Between Charlie and the graves were wounded men. Thousands of them. Blank-eyed men who might not have recognized their own mothers, wives, or sisters had they stopped by for a how-do-you-do. But then, their families might not have recognized them either. Some were still; some writhed in pain. All were packed together with barely a path between the them, head to head, toe to toe, back to back. Except for the moans from unconscious men, and the buzz of insects, there was a quiet about the place. No one called out for help. Instead, they waited.

Millions of flies buzzed about. Few men had the strength to brush them away. Above, the sun was veiled with billions of bits of sand and earth kicked up by the shelling and bombs. Everything was gray and bleak. Even the blood was a dull, lifeless purple.

It was more than Charlie could take in.

"Where's the . . ." Charlie's voice faltered, "doctor."

"Down there."

Turning back to the house, Charlie spotted a hole in the wall. Beside the wall were bales of hay. He crouched down, and in the gloom, saw a sloping ramp that ran down to what once might have been a cellar. One step on the ramp and Charlie slipped. He rolled, head over heels, to the bottom. The wall at the bottom stopped him short and he near knocked himself senseless.

Two small rooms — caves, really, with rounded, brick ceilings and connected by a small passageway — served as the operating room and post-operating room. Hay was scattered over the floor, dampened down with blood.

Hunched over a table in one of the rooms, lit only by a dangling lamp from above and a few stubby candles that had been jammed into crevices in the wall, Dr. Robert Daniels worked.

"Sir," he whispered, "Excuse . . ."

No one paid him any mind.

Charlie, dizzy and rubbing the back of his head, shrank down against the wall to sit on his haunches. He waited. Soldiers were carried in and out with breathtaking speed. It wasn't operations that were taking place, more wraps, jabs, and patches. Occasionally a leg or arm had to come off — no choice. There was no anesthetic.

Great, silent tears rolled down Charlie's face. "Please, God, if you are listening, stop this," he whispered.

"Doctor, tea?" The medic held out a cup of tea.

"Thank you." Dr. Daniels pointed to a makeshift wash-basin and the orderly set it down on the edge. A stretcher-bearer removed his last patient. Dr. Daniels turned and plunged his hands in water.

"Dr. Daniels?"

"Yes."

"Dr. Daniels, it's me — Charlie Wilcox." Charlie bounced up and stood straight and tall. He wiped his face with the back of his hand making a path through the mud on his face.

Dr. Daniels looked at Charlie while drying his hands. There was no sign of recognition.

"Charlie Wilcox, from St. John's. I was in the General Hospital. I had my foot fixed. You carried my friend Davy down the hall and . . . Mac." Charlie stopped to catch his breath.

"In all the world . . ." Dr. Robert Daniels stood, his mouth agape. "Charlie, I . . ." He was at a loss for words.

"Dr. Daniels," the medic motioned to the operating table. A wild-eyed boy looked back from the table. "What's your name, son?" Dr. Daniels asked the boy. "Dale, sir, Jimmy Dale, from Bay Roberts."

"Know it well."

"Dr. Daniels, I have a message for you . . ." Charlie danced beside Dr. Daniels.

The medic came around the table and hustled Charlie out. "It's from Mac," Charlie yelled over his shoulder. But Dr. Daniels heard only the boy's cry and saw only the wound in front of him.

Charlie found himself back out in the sunlight. Nothing was accomplished, nothing at all. He picked up a water bottle that was lying on the ground, filled it up from the well, and stumbled back through the maze of wounded. Charlie held the bottle to Martin's lips and let the water trickle in bit by bit.

"No problem, Martin. The doctor will see you soon. But here's how it is, you can't get dehydrated. That means you have to drink water. And I'm going to have to keep your wounds clean, OK?"

Charlie set to work using everything he had learned in the hospital to keep Martin alive, and then some. He rigged a shelter out of the butt of a gun, a stick, and an old sheet he scrounged. It would keep the sun off. Draped gently over Martin's face, it would also keep the flies at bay. But the sun or the flies were not Charlie's worry — a chilly night was. All the while, Charlie talked. About home, about fishing, about Davy, and Claire, and his best friend, Jim Norton, and about Clint, too. "He's a bully, all right. But he'll never get me again, Martin, that's sure. And you know, I'll never get him." Charlie looked out over the carnage of war. "Does no good to fight. There's got to be another way."

Time went by. Hundreds more wounded filled up the pasture. It was a never-ending stream of misery.

Charlie dribbled more water into Martin's mouth. "I'm going to leave you for a bit. I need to talk to the doctor again. Martin, squeeze my hand if you can hear me." Nothing. "Martin!" Charlie yelled. Then he felt a light touch to his hand. "That's good. Think about Meeta, Martin. Think about home."

Charlie set off again, this time with a sure step. He ran around the back of the farmhouse and ducked into the basement. Dr. Daniels was still standing at the operating table. He would have done hundreds of operations this day.

"Dr. Daniels," said Charlie, not loudly, but with authority.

"That's enough, boy," the medic said sharply.

"It's all right. Take this one out." Dr. Daniels motioned to the boy on the table and turned back to the washbasin. Again he plunged his hands into hot water.

"Can you come outside with me? There is someone . . . my friend . . ." Charlie lost his confidence. "Please," was all he could say. Tears ran down his face, and there was no way to stop them. "Please," Charlie whispered. "Please."

Dr. Daniels paused. He looked at Charlie square in the face. "Medic, what time is it?"

"Almost 3:00, doctor. You've been working for fourteen hours."

"Day or night?" asked the doctor.

"Day."

Dr. Daniels looked back to the medic and said, "I'm going up for some air and something to eat. I'll be back in ten minutes."

The two went up into the light. Dr. Daniels staggered, then caught himself from falling. He looked over the field of wounded men. He said nothing. The distant guns were strangely quiet.

"I'll look at your friend, Charlie," Dr. Daniels said quietly.

Charlie near cried out for joy. "This way, this way." Charlie picked through the soldiers lying on the ground. It was a hard slog. Hands reached out to Dr. Daniels and he stopped often to say a word, to touch a soldier. Efforts by the stretcher-bearers to make little paths, inroads to the wounded, had failed as one soldier, then another, flailed about.

At last they came to Martin.

"His name is Martin, Private Martin." And Charlie stopped. In all this time, in all they had been through, Charlie didn't know Martin's last name! He might have laughed. "I don't know his last name, but he's my friend."

Dr. Daniels undid Martin's coat. He examined the wound in Martin's side and the gash on his leg.

"Charlie, come here," Dr. Daniels motioned to Charlie, and the two stood out of Martin's earshot. "He needs an operation, Charlie, and this is no place for it. And even with the operation, it doesn't look good."

"You can do it though, can't you?" Charlie's heart was near froze. Martin would make it, Charlie knew it. All he needed was help.

"Look around, Charlie. If I spend an hour on him, I lose two or three others."

Charlie had no words or tears. He just looked at Dr. Daniels and prayed to himself.

"Oh, Charlie," Dr. Daniels let out a long, slow breath. "All right, tell you what. Keep him alive till nightfall. Another doctor will relieve me. I'll do the operation then. Keep the wounds clean, keep him warm, and keep the liquid in him." Dr. Daniels began to walk back to the farmhouse. "And, Charlie, look around. There are others who need your help, too. If you're going to wear that band, live up to its name." He walked away.

Charlie turned back to Martin and made his clothes right. "I forgot," said Charlie to no one in particular, "to tell him about the baby."

Charlie worked. He collected scrub, and bits of wood, to build a small fire. He cleaned and bound wounds as best he could. He filled up water bottles, and helped those wounded who wanted to sit up. He fetched tea from the makeshift canteen and held the cups up to open mouths. He arranged men around the fire and then he stripped the dead. Coats from corpses were used to keep the living warm. Reaching into tunics, he found field dressing kits and put them to use.

"Medic," said a voice. "Could you help me?"

Charlie leaned over a boy, not much older than himself. His face was streaked with mud, and his body was as rigid as a plank of wood.

"If I can," said Charlie softly.

"My coat. My coat. Could you, would you mind?" was all he could say.

Charlie lifted the coat off the boy. It was alive with lice.

Charlie touched the boy's shoulder. "I'll have you fixed in a jiffy."

THE SUN SET, and even the flies settled. Dr. Daniels, true to his word, arrived with two stretcher-bearers in tow.

"You've done a fine job, Charlie," he said, looking about. He pointed to Martin. The stretcher-bearers quickly shifted Martin onto a litter and made their way back to the farmhouse. Charlie set out to follow.

"Stay here, Charlie. I don't need you in there, but they need you out here. And Charlie," Dr. Daniels turned and faced him, "you can be proud of what you have done."

Charlie nodded dumbly as he watched Martin and the little troupe disappear in the dark.

CHARLIE SPENT THE NIGHT tending the fire and the sick. He rubbed his arms. It was a cold night and he was hungry. What he wouldn't give for a taste of figgy duff. Charlie laughed out loud.

"What ya laughing at, boy?" A soldier, himself propped up on his elbow, looked over at Charlie.

"I was thinking," said Charlie, "that I was in the mood for a taste of me mother's figgy duff."

The soldier roared with laughter. "With a splash of sunny sauce, I'll wager."

AS DAWN BROKE, Charlie was slumped in a heap. He stuck his hands deep into his pockets and fingered a piece of paper. Out came Davy's drawing of Mac and, along with it, Michael's letter and Bible. The letter wasn't sealed, the trenches not being a place with spare envelopes.

Charlie unfolded the letter, careful like, and read it.

Dear Mother,

It is just hours before what they call the Big Push. If you read this, then it is certain I have not survived the battle. I want you to know that I am surrounded by the best of men, not a shirker amongst them. Good Newfoundland lads, Mother, as good friends as I have ever known.

My last thoughts should be of prayer, but all I can think of is you. I can see you sitting on the edge of my bed, Mother, singing to me. I see your hair shining in the light and your gentle face.

A boy never had a finer mother as you. I think of all you did for me, and I am sorry I will not be there in body, to care for you in your old age. If God allows it, I will be with you in spirit. I love you, Mother, I do that.

Your faithful son,
Michael

Charlie folded the letter up, tucked it safely in Michael's Bible, and put it back in his pocket.

IT WAS NOTHING in particular that woke him, but wake he did, and with a start. Two soldiers were doing their best to walk about, taking long strides, then short ones, being careful not to step on the wounded.

"Have you seen or heard of Tom Westway, Private Westway?" asked one.

Charlie shook his head.

"Westway, Westway," shouted the man as he walked away.

"It's his brother he's after," said the second soldier to Charlie. "Cig?"

Charlie shook his head. "What's the date?"

"July 2. Expect July 1 will be a day to be remembered."

"Have they taken a head count yet?"

"Took roll call an hour back," replied the soldier. "Sixty-eight accounted for."

"How m-many," stuttered Charlie, "how many went over the top?"

"Of the Newfoundland boys — eight hundred, or thereabouts." And the soldier walked away with his chin tucked into his tunic.

Charlie fell back into what passed for a sleep. He dreamed about the anchor again — the steel anchor that kept floating to the top of the water. It bobbed there like a detached buoy.

"YOU THE ONE THAT brought in the soldier with the bum leg and a hole in his side?" A grim-faced medic stood behind Charlie.

"Yes, yes, that was me." Charlie nodded and rubbed his face with his hands. The sun was coming up and the dew was on the grass, war or no war.

"He's been put in a lorry ambulance. He's going on to the hospital, and back to Blighty after that, I'll wager. He's a lucky beggar."

Charlie leaped up. "Where's the ambulance?"

"Over there." Sure enough, off in the distance, a lorry was being loading up with the wounded. Dr. Daniels was barking out commands like the Colonel himself. Charlie ran. Ran and ran and ran.

"Dr. Daniels, is he all right?" Charlie stopped so fast he near plowed into the side of the lorry.

"He'll make it, Charlie. You were right. He had the will," said Dr. Daniels.

"His leg?"

"He's got both, but he'll have a limp. He's out of this war."

"Thank you, thank you." Charlie gulped. "I have something to tell you."

"Not now, Charlie. Driver, ready?" Dr. Daniels hollered.

"No, it's . . ." Charlie ran up beside him.

"Get in the lorry, Charlie. This is no place for you. And get yourself home. You hear? Home, Charlie. Newfoundland. Go to school. Be with your people. Get in there."

Charlie scrambled up into the back of the ambulance lorry. "Listen to me," Charlie was near ready to blow a gasket. "It's about Mac. Mac, Lily. Your wife!" And in a voice that sang above the roar of the engine, "She is going to have a baby!"

Dr. Daniels stopped dead, like a northern gale just froze him in his tracks. "Hold it, driver."

He stood, dumbfounded.

"It's true," Charlie smiled. "You're going to be a father."

Dr. Robert Daniels smiled. He laughed out loud. "A baby." And he laughed all over again. And then he pulled himself up short. "How is Lily? She must go home."

"She is going home. I had a ticket. I gave it to her. I know she'll take it because she knows that she'll lose the baby if she doesn't. Besides, it would have gone to waste." Charlie grinned. "It's July 2. She'll be in London now boarding the ship. It leaves today."

"Charlie," sputtered Dr. Daniels, "I don't know what to say."

The driver poked his head around the corner of the lorry. "Time to go, doctor."

"And one more thing," said Charlie, as he fumbled in his pockets. "Here, this is for you." Dr. Daniels took the paper from Charlie's hand and unfolded it. It was the drawing of Mac.

Dr. Daniels held it in both hands. "It's . . . it's . . . beautiful. You?"

"No, I didn't draw it. Davy did it. Remember him? From the hospital in St. John's?"

Dr. Daniels nodded as he fingered the paper. "And you carried it, all along . . ." Dr. Daniels sputtered. "You can't know what this means to me, Charlie. And I think I know what it means to you too."

"That's it, doc!" a medic called out from inside the lorry.

"Go," he yelled to the driver. And to Charlie, "Thank you. Thank you. Now get home, Charlie. Have a good life."

As the lorry pulled away, Charlie yelled out, "And she thinks it's a girl."

"A house full of girls," yelled Dr. Daniels, his legs running after the lorry without his say-so. "That's what we'll have. A house full of girls, just as beautiful as their mother."

Dr. Daniels stopped and waved, and for a small moment there was no war.

CHARLIE PLUNKED HIMSELF down on the ambulance floor beside Martin's stretcher.

"I want to thank you, too, Charlie," Martin coughed.

"You awake? How do you feel?" Charlie put his hand on Martin's forehead. His temperature was down. "Hey, medic, lend me your watch." Charlie caught the watch with one hand and took up Martin's wrist with the other, feeling for his pulse.

"What you did . . . I can't recall it all now, but I will and . . ." Martin's eyes wanted to close. He fought hard to keep them open.

"Not bad," said Charlie as he handed the watch back to the medic.

"What about Michael? Did he make it?"

Charlie pulled Michael's Bible from his pocket and laid it on Martin's chest. Martin flung his arm over it and pressed it to him. "He's safe now," Martin whispered, "in heaven, for sure this must be hell."

"No talking," Charlie adjusted the rough blanket that

covered Martin. "It's going to work out. They'll not send you back, not with a bad leg and that hole in your side. And Mac will go home and have her baby, and Dr. Daniels will come home too." Charlie sat back and took a deep breath, like he hadn't taken a breath in days. "And I will sail the world. I know that now. And . . . oh, Jeeze!" Like a shot in the head.

"Driver, stop! Stop!" Charlie pummeled the back wall of the lorry. The vehicle came to a screeching halt.

"Martin, listen good." Charlie spoke fast. "I've got to go back. I forgot something. There's a letter in the Bible. See that Michael's mother gets it."

Martin rose up and grabbed Charlie's arm. "No, you're not going anywhere but home."

"I got to. I forgot something important, something I promised never to lose. I have to go find it. Take care, Martin."

The back door of the lorry flew open, and out came Charlie, running full tilt back to the trenches.

"Charlie, no." Martin yelled as loud as he could.

It was no good. Charlie was barreling down the road like the enemy was at his back, not in front of him.

Chapter 22

"It's some soup out there." Claire arranged herself on a rock. "How can you see anything?"

"I can see all right," said Jim Norton. He held up a pair of binoculars and scanned the horizon for the millionth time. Jim flopped down on the hill, the very same hill that he and Charlie sat on more than three years ago.

"Just because you've been down to the Labrador doesn't mean you have the eyes of a captain. Anyway, how do you know he's coming home this week?" asked Claire.

"The letter said . . ."

"I know full well what the letter said, Jim Norton. It said that Charlie was wounded, but it didn't say how bad. It said that he was a medic with Lily's husband, Dr. Dan something."

"Daniels." Jim loved correcting Claire Guy.

"I wish Lily and the baby had stayed longer. It was nice having a baby around," said Claire wistfully.

"You could always go visit her in St. John's," Jim suggested hopefully. He was always looking for a way to get rid of Claire.

"Maybe," said Claire. "Do you think it's true? About Charlie, I mean. Do you think he really traveled to all those battles as Dr. Daniels' assistant?"

"Yes, I think it's true," said Jim with a smile. "He was at Cambrai, Passchendale, went to Paris and London, too. Did lots more I expect."

"Well, the war's been over for months now. It's time he came home," said Claire smartly. "Do you think he's wounded real bad?"

"Maybe."

"Samuel MacLeod came home from the war with one arm gone," said Claire. "Blown clean off. And part of his head, too. Missus Lamb said he wasn't right in the head to begin with so that part didn't matter much. Shame about the arm though."

"Listen . . ." Jim cocked his head like a small dog. Claire did the same.

"I don't . . ."

"Quiet." If you were real quiet, sometimes you could hear a ship coming in before you could see it.

"I still don't . . ." And then she could. And then she ran, down the hill and into the village.

"He's coming. He's coming." Like a town crier. "Charlie. Charlie is coming home."

Claire Guy flew into Lucy's house and hollered down the hall. "Missus Lucy, there's a ship comin' in." Claire clutched her side and tried to catch her breath.

"What's the racket about?" Emma Fields came clumping down the stairs, kicking her black mourning skirt ahead of her. She may never have gotten the chance to marry that thick Murphy Milford, but she'd darn well get the respect due an engaged woman of a fallen soldier. Just like him to get himself killed.

"A ship's come in." Claire puffed.

"And what surprise is there in that?" said Emma, as she landed on the last step. "Brigus is a harbor."

"Oh never mind. Missus Lucy. Missus Lucy," Emma yelled up the stairs, "It's here."

The words were no more out her mouth when Charlie's mother charged down the stairs, near knocking Emma senseless. She was running, running as fast as she had ever run in her life. She was thirteen years old again and racing to win at the church picnic. She was sixteen and running to meet her own dad as he put down anchor after a half year at sea. She was thirty-five years old and running for all her life to hold her son.

Sam came barreling out the house right behind her, bits of shaving cream still around his ears, and his shirttail hanging out. The two made it to the docks in no time. The ship weighed anchor.

"It's him, Sam, it's got to be him," Lucy whispered.

"Hang on, darling. We've been disappointed before." Sam stood behind his wife, his arms circling her. It was Claire who had brought the Wilcoxes, but Jim, too, had run about, hollering Charlie's arrival. A small group gathered, Missus Fox, Mister Lambe with Missus Lambe hot on his heels.

The ship's anchor crashed down into the water. Thick ropes were flung down from the port and stern. It took the men on shore no time, none a'tall, to secure the ship. The gangplank landed with a bang, and then a muffled thud.

The captain stood on deck, his arms folded. It wasn't often he put into harbor in Brigus.

"Charlie," Lucy whispered. Nothing. "Charlie," Lucy called out as loud as she possibly could. "Charlie." Nothing. "Please, Charlie."

He wasn't there, he wasn't on board. Lucy turned around and buried her face in Sam's shoulder.

"He's not there, Sam. He's not there. I want him home, Sam. I want my boy back." Lucy's body was wracked with sobs. Three years, three long years and then some, he had been away. And every moment he had been in danger.

"I don't think you'll ever get your boy back, Lucy," Skipper Sam whispered into her ear. "He's gone forever."

"What? What are you saying?" Lucy looked up at her husband in horror.

"Turn around, love."

Lucy turned. She looked past the man in front of her, then back again. There stood Charlie. Tall, grown, a man.

"Charlie?" Lucy said softly. She reached out and gently touched his scruffy beard.

Everything about him was strong and sure. Like his father.

"Mother." Charlie reached out for his mother. Sam wrapped his arms around them both.

"Charlie, Charlie," Lucy sobbed, over and over.

It was Sam who spotted the spy glass sticking out from Charlie's pack.

"You didn't lose it?" Sam threw his head back and laughed.

"Never." Charlie looked into his father's eyes, eyes the color of fog rolling in from the bay.

Jim Norton stood off to the side, waiting for his turn.

"Jim," Charlie cried. They stopped short of flinging their arms around each other and instead shook hands and laughed like they'd never stop.

It was then that Charlie noticed her.

"Who's that?" Charlie whispered to Jim. He pointed to the girl running full tilt back into the village.

"Get off, it's only Claire."

"That's Claire? Where is she going?"

"Who knows? Don't mind that now, Charlie," Jim laughed and walloped him on the back. "Yer home."

Charlie smiled back and gazed around. He felt the rock-hard ground beneath his feet. He looked into the faces of those he'd known all his life. He was home.

Fact or Fiction?

Fact and fiction are companions. Charlie Wilcox was born weighing two pounds, with a club foot, in the village of Brigus, Newfoundland. Charlie's father, Captain Samuel Wilcox was considered to be one of the finest captains Brigus has ever produced. He commanded many ships, the most famous was the *Thetis*.

Charlie did, indeed, have an operation on his club foot. He did punch out a kid without legs while he was in the hospital. It was a burden (his words) that he carried to his death. He also sailed, as cabin boy, around the world with Captain Robert (Bob) Bartlett. He did not go to war.

Charlie, who died during the writing of this story, loved it. But what would he think of his great niece shipping him off to war? "Truth is a nice thing, but don't let it get in the way of a good story," he said. Spoken like a true Newfoundlander.

Postscript

On July 1, 1916, at the Battle of the Somme, Beaumont Hamel sector, the Newfoundland Regiment proved themselves to be among the bravest soldiers in the world. Lieutenant-General Sir Aylmer Hunter-Weston, the Commander of the Seventh Corps at the Battle of the Somme, described this dedicated collection of men as, "Better Than the Best." And that was true. The regiment went on to distinguish themselves and, by the end of the war, were given the title *Royal* Newfoundland Regiment.

Every effort was made to stay true to, if not Charlie's story, then the history of the time. There is one notable exception. Ships carrying troops from North America to England would have docked in Liverpool, on the west coast of England, and not London.

Did You Know?

angishore — weak, puny fellow, unlucky, too lazy to fish. It is often pronounced by "hangashore."

back house — a storage room, often found in homes around the ports of Newfoundland. It was attached to the backdoor of the home, and served as a porch.

bayman (bayboy) — derogatory term for a man who lives in the outports of Newfoundland.

berth — a place on board a ship with, in the case of sealing, a share in the ship's profits.

Blighty — slang word for England used during both world wars but more commonly in World War I.

brewis — a favorite Newfoundlander's meal of salt cod and hard tack (hard bread). (*See also* hard tack.)

bully beef — bits of tinned beef swimming in grease, a staple for the common soldiers in the front lines. It was usually eaten directly out of the tin.

burnt — a part of the body so frozen with the cold, it's as if it were burnt by fire.

chisels — thin metal straps driven into the heel of a shoe of a sealer's boot to prevent him from slipping on the ice.

cookee — a cook's assistant on ships heading to the ice or down to the Labrador coopy down — to crouch, squat, or bend down low to the ground.

corner boy — derogatory term for a St. John's man or boy, used by someone who might live in the outports. Lazy, someone with nothing better to do than stand on a corner. (*See also* townie.)

dog hood — adult hood seal. Vicious, as strong as a bull, it does not run away but will defend its family.

duckboard — wooden planks laid on the ground.

FANY — First Aid Nursing Yeomanry Corps.

figgy duff — a pudding, often served alongside the main meal, but occasionally eaten as a dessert. It's made with flour, molasses, raisins, cinnamon, and cloves, and is topped with a brown sugar sauce.

gaff hook — iron rod used to kill or stun a seal. Also used as a walking stick on the ice pans.

gaffer — boy in the fishing industry, usually between ten and fifteen years old. Helped out and assisted fishermen.

hard tack — thick, oval-shaped biscuits. They should be soaked in water for several hours before eating. Sometimes called sea-biscuit. (*See also* brewis.)

haversack — a backpack. (*See also* kitbag.)

infantry — foot soldier.

jig (as in "jig a few fish") — to fish with an unbaited, weighted hook.

jinker — someone who brings bad luck.

kitbag — soldier's bag, usually tube shaped. (*See also* haversack.)

lop souce — watery stew.

mackintosh — rain coat.

muddle — wooden stirring spoon shaped like miniature

shovel.

over the top — climbing out of the trenches.

pan — a small piece of flat ice, usually circular. A sealer, or child, would leap from ice pan to ice pan.

pisspot — another name for chamber pots.

quintals — a hundred weight (112 pounds or 50.8 kg.), a measure of cod-fish caught by a fisherman.

sealing box — small, rectangular, wooden box that holds a sealer's personal effects.

sleeveens — rogue, rascal. A sly, deceitful man. A mean fellow or a mischievous child.

sloucher — someone who does not do his duty, lazy.

shrapnel — fragments from an exploding shell.

shilling — a silver coin worth around 20 cents. Used before Newfoundland joined Canada.

shinnicked — numbed and paralyzed with the cold.

sniper — a person who fires a gun from a hiding place.

sparable — a short nail or cleat that is used as a stud in the heel of a boot or shoe.

ticket — an authorized place or berth on a sealing ship. The tickets are handed out by captains or officers. Along with a ticket came a *crop note* which was worth, at the time, approximately $10.00, and was to be spent on supplies at the local store. Sealers might buy a suit of oilskins, boots, food (oatmeal, sugar, raisins, and so on), tin cup, gloves, tobacco, and such.

townie — a Newfoundlander who lives in St. John's or in a town away from the coast. (*See also* corner boy.)

Ulsterman — a person from the province of Ulster, Northern Ireland.